# FRONTIER RATS

## QUEST FOR RATOPIA

I. Pirrie

www.frontierrats.com

ISBN-13: 978-1548311704

ISBN-10: 1548311707

**Library of Congress
Control Number: 2017910288
CreateSpace Independent Publishing
Platform, North Charleston, SC**

# INTRODUCTION

After the great global environmental disaster planet Earth was thrown into a mini ice age. Only the hardiest creatures survived. The rats who did survive remember the details only too well. Another terrible bit of history that the humans brought about.

Grumthorpe city is surrounded by barren wastelands with the threat of death at every turn. Rats and humans compete for food or space and this presents the humans with a big problem. Typically they opt for their usual solution: extermination!

The rats are left with only one escape, to stow away aboard a spaceship bound for a distant galaxy in the hope of finding safe refuge on an alien planet. When every enemy is larger than you, ferocious aliens, killer cyborg cats, mad scientists and a hateful human crew you have to be smart to survive. But will their self-serving rat ways bring about their own extinction?

# Chapter 1

## TWIGS

In a sunny meadow under an endless blue sky, insects buzz and zizz in the tall, waving grass and birds warble in the distant hedgerows. Uphrasia Teach, a young common brown rat lies on his back bathing in the sun, a thing rats love to do. He is slim with a long snout, smooth brown fur, dark tips to his ears and a dark tuft of hair in the middle of his forehead above his dark bushy eyebrows. With his paws behind his head and his eyes closed, he breathes softly. "Ah, this is the life. All this and as many fresh slugs as I can fit in my tummy. Pure paradise!"

*The common brown rat (Rattus Norvegicus) is believed to have originated from Asia. They are the most successful mammal in the world after humans. There is a saying: "Wherever you are asleep or awake, there's a common brown rat ten feet from your head!"*

A voice nearby rudely awakens him back to reality. "Hey Uphrasia wake up! You've had your four hours already."

Grumthorpe city is crowded with sooty skyscrapers and choking motorways that wind around under and over each other. Cars and trucks move slowly in long fume-belching queues making the atmosphere barely breathable. Smoking chimneys and factories share space with residential tower blocks. A constant grey cloud of smog hangs over this overcrowded city. You wouldn't hang your washing out here. Beyond the city to the north, east and south is an endless wasteland. The soil is so barren that nothing grows save for a few hardy shrubs and weeds like dandelion, stinging nettle and thistle. To the west is the black dead forest that spreads out for about five miles and is then interrupted by more deserted wasteland.

Snow falls over the black hills and down into the forest valley where a granite quarry has been carved out to contain the old Grumthorpe municipal sewage plant. The gate is permanently open to a short drive that leads over to a flat roof with a stubby lookout tower sitting on the top. Most of its windows are boarded up with wooden planks. Lines of long copper pipes lead down from the plant to thirty round steaming filter beds. The pipes terminate over tanks of raw sewage which is pumped along metal arms that rotate and trickle the grey oozy liquid over the filter rocks below. What a stink! – like rotten eggs combined with the smelliest feet you've ever had the misfortune to smell. Underneath the sewage plant is a vast network of tunnels and passages that lead to long-abandoned cellars and storerooms. Lines of wooden pigeon-holes are precariously stacked from floor to ceiling with tiny ladders next to them. These are the rats' sleeping quarters and because they only need a few hours' sleep at a time they sleep in shifts. In one of these cramped little boxes Uphrasia yawns and puts on his grey cotton Space Corps tunic. The collar is frayed and there is a patch on one side. He stretches. "Is it time already? Can't I have one more hour? I was having such a splendid dream."

Another rat in a matching tunic pokes his head in. "You know the rules. Get up it's my turn!"

Uphrasia scratches his tummy. "Back to the grind then." He climbs out of the box as the other rat hops in and plumps the pillow. Uphrasia descends the ladder and joins a slow-moving queue of rats at the bottom of a long corridor. There are many types of rat in the line: brown and black rat, fancy rat, albino and the elite genetically bred tan-brown Zucker rats. They all look at the floor as they move forward a pace at a time. Uphrasia thinks to himself. "This is a far cry from the great Gorgonzola's vision of Ratopia. I bet he'd turn in his cage if he could see how we live now."

A short, tubby brown rat joins him, his tunic has lost a couple of buttons where his belly bulges. He has a short tuft of hair between his ears and two large front teeth. He smiles up at Uphrasia with beady black eyes and nudges him in the ribs. "Morning, face ache. Foraging day. Hey, hey!"

"Oh joy of joys, foraging. I suppose it's better than a shift on the maggot farm. Morning Konrad."

"Maggots! Oh I don't like them. A nice hot slug that's the ticket!"

"Well you're in luck as slugs are on the menu today. They are on the menu every day. Except maggot Monday."

The queue terminates in a large dilapidated kitchen full of chattering rats sitting at a miss-matched collection of paw-made tables. The walls are covered with white tiles and a huge extractor hood hangs from the ceiling. The din of the chattering rats is so loud everyone has to shout to be heard. Beneath a high white butler's sink is a long makeshift counter covered in dishes of slugs, fried worms and boiled beetles. Uphrasia and Konrad each take a white yoghurt pot lid and move along the serving counter. A tall female dinner rat picks up a hot steaming brown slug with tongs and places it on Konrad's lid. He looks up at her and frowns and she tilts her head to one side. "Is there something wrong young rat?"

"May I have another slug, please?"

The dinner rat forces a half smile picks up a clipboard flips over a page and reads out loud. "Konrad Konstantin! On diet rations. You have to lose six grams!"

Konrad's shoulders drop and the sides of his mouth turn down. "Six whole grams! That's half an average rat!" He moves along and another serving rat plonks a pile of crispy fried worms on his lid. Konrad sniffs them then trudges over to the end of a table and takes a seat.

Uphrasia moves up and the dinner rat places three plump slugs on his pot lid. He frowns and she folds her arms and scowls. "Too skinny!" Uphrasia squeezes into the space next to Konrad, then puts one of his slugs on Konrad's lid.

"Thanks buddy. Are you sure?"

"Yeah, probably full of slug pellets anyway."

Konrad picks up a slug and gulps it down in one mouthful. He is distracted by a noise from another table and looks over his shoulder. A group of tall sandy-brown Zucker rats in smart shiny silver uniforms are acting up. Uphrasia looks over. "Huh! Zucker rats! So-called elite cadets! Just because they were genetically bred to be fitter, smarter and faster than us doesn't mean they are better than us."

"Well, technically speaking it does." Konrad chomps on the crispy worms.

*The Zucker rat was specially bred by scientists for use in laboratories. They were genetically selected for their high intelligence and agility. They have short, light-tan fur which is very smooth.*

A paper cup hits Uphrasia on the back of the head. "What the?!"

A tall, slim Zucker rat Roderick stands up. "Hey Uphrasia! What's that perfume you're wearing?! Is it ca-ca de Canal?!"

All the rats in the room laugh then a tall beefy Zucker rat Thompus joins in. "No, it's odour de toilet! Ha-ha-ha!"

All the rats roll around laughing. Uphrasia stands up. "It's a very old joke and not that funny!" He pats Konrad on the back. "Come on Konrad let's get a head start on foraging." Konrad stifles his own laughter gets up and follows him.

Grumthorpe Forest is a dark and gloomy place. Patches of thin, dry grass are interrupted by areas of barren, brown mud. All the trees are leafless and coated in black soot; some are hollow and house various forest dwellers. Bats hang upside down in the uppermost branches, blinking and scratching, waiting for sunset so they can begin their night hunting for airborne bugs. A barn owl glides silently on the wind, then darts out into a clearing and down into the waving grass. It rises up clutching a small vole in its talons, then flaps off into the trees and vanishes. Below the twisting roots of a great oak is a mound of soil excavated by badgers.

Six rats march in a line along the snow-covered path; at the back are Uphrasia and Konrad. They stop in front of a tall, stocky black rat: General Scrod. He is in his mid-fours with thick black fur and wears a smart, dark-green military jacket with shiny polished buttons. There are a few grey whiskers on his snout and he has dark steely eyes. The young rats chatter among themselves. Scrod frowns at them until they all go quiet. "Good evening cadets!" His breath makes puffs of vapour in the frosty air. "Welcome to my course in nature foraging. I am General Scrod!" He paces left and right in front of the group. "Some of you may be content with slug rations, sharing a bed with the unwashed and living in a sewer for the rest of your lives. But some of you, some of you may have a bigger idea! Adventure!" His wide eyes stare at them. "A life of exploration, danger and discovery!"

*The black rat (Rattus rattus) came to our lands after stowing away aboard ships. Also known as the ship rat or old English rat, they are the fiercest and boldest of all the rats.*

Scrod looks around the forest and holds out his paws. "The wilderness is a dangerous and challenging place, but it can provide you with all the food and shelter you need if you have the correct training. Now follow me and let's see who has the aptitude for forest survival!" He turns abruptly, marches off and they follow in line. At the front and looking very keen is Rose, a fancy rat with several brown and black patches over clean white fur and two neat brown lines down her snout. She is a little taller than the other

12

rats and has bright brown eyes with delicate lashes. She rubs her cold paws together and blows on them.

*Fancy rats were bred to be pets, and, although they occasionally nip your finger, they are very tame and friendly to humans. They come in all sorts of colours with different patches and patterns. Their good nature makes them very popular with other rats.*

Scrod reaches a fallen branch and the group gather round him in a semicircle as he tips it over, leans down and picks up a wriggling white grub. "Here we go. This is a common find under rotted wood or leaf mulch." He bites it in half and shows it to them. Green gooey slime drips from its writhing body. "Anyone want to try?"

Rose covers her mouth. "Yuck!"

Konrad is about to step forward but Uphrasia holds out his paw and shakes his head.

"That bad huh?"

"Worse!"

Scrod shrugs and throws the rest of the grub up into the air, catches it in his mouth and chews. "Right, let's move on. Split up into pairs and forage for an hour, then bring what you find back here for inspection. Off you go and remember, steer clear of humans!" Konrad raises his paw. Scrod scowls down at him. "Well speak up lad, what is it?"

"Sir, are there any dangerous predators in the forest?"

"Predators? No, nothing to worry yourself about young fella." He pats Konrad on the head. "Nothing at all." As the recruits disperse in pairs, Scrod scratches his chin. "Unless of course you count foxes or badgers, hawks, owls, stoats and weasels. Then there's bats, polecats, three-toed sloths, bears, cougars, bandicoots, flibber gibbers and grottle flaggers! Come to think of it, I think I'll hide out in that hollow tree over there until you all get back." With that he scampers off towards a hollow tree and hops inside, then pokes his snout out through a hole.

The foragers climb up a slope, spread out and search through the undergrowth, tipping over logs and kicking up leaf litter. Rose has partnered up with a small, thin rat named Scout. He is also a fancy rat and has one single brown patch on his back with several smaller spots around his waist and a round patch over his left eye. He picks up a squirming centipede and frowns. "General Scr-Scrod is very sc-scary." The centipede wriggles and writhes in his paw.

Rose smiles warmly. "He seems like a bit of a grump. I'm sure he has a soft side once you get to know him."

Scout throws down the centipede and continues to search in the leaf mulch. "Well I wouldn't want to get on his b-bad side, I can tell you."

Rose picks up the end of a long, flat piece of tree bark. "Here, give me a paw." Scout grabs the other end and they tip it over. Hundreds of woodlice and tiny beetles scurry about. Scout hops forward and grabs an enormous beetle. "Are you sure you can manage that?" Rose raises her eyebrows.

"Argh! Yes, I'm taking this back to the General." He wrestles with the beetle.

Konrad kicks aside a pile of leaves then looks up at Uphrasia. "You're not foraging?"

Uphrasia stands with his paws on his hips. "What's the point? We'll never get selected to go on a mission. Only those elite cadets get to go on an adventure. This is a total waste of my time. I'm going to visit Mother."

Konrad's jaw drops. "But what about sticking together, foraging, the General? He'll get really mad!"

"It's the Rat Way buddy."

Konrad's shoulders droop. "Every rat for himself."

"You've got it. Now cover for me, I'll see you later." He saunters off leaving Konrad shaking his head.

Uphrasia puffs as he climbs the steep lane that curves around a bend rising up Weary Rodent Hill. The light is fading and the overhanging trees make the lane dark. An owl hoots in the distance and he stops to listen, sniffs the fresh, cool forest air, and when he is sure all is safe he moves on up the slope. He slithers

15

through a crack in the concrete kerb, into a cramped round tunnel that goes along level for about a foot then rises up steeply. The den is small and cosy, with a few crude sticks of furniture. A small fire burns in a hearth cut out of the clay wall. Overhead the roots of a tree have been woven together to make a strong ceiling and a single wooden beam keeps it all in place. The walls have been pounded hard as stone and covered with a fine floral wallpaper. A number of small framed pictures are hung with family images. In the centre hangs a large framed picture of Uphrasia as a baby rat on a beach sitting proudly next to a big sand castle in the shape of a giant wedge of cheese.

Uphrasia's mother Margaret, a plump brown rat with grey whiskers, hums cheerfully to herself. She is wearing an apron and head scarf and is stirring a rusty paint tin filled with porridge oats over an old oil lamp. She speaks with a strong Scottish accent. "Is that you my dear? Sit down. I had a feeling you'd be arriving. No doubt you're hungry."

Uphrasia nuzzles her on the cheek and sits at the table made out of an old upturned Frisbee on legs, which is very handy as nothing ever spills on the floor. She places a wooden bowl of porridge in front of him and he shovels a big spoonful into his mouth with a wooden spoon. "You're looking thin, my boy." She strokes the tuft between his ears. "Are they feeding you properly at that dreadful establishment?"

He quickly wolfs down the porridge and nods. "Yes Mother, I'm eating just fine."

She wrings her paws together. "I do worry about you at that ridiculous astro school. Promise me you won't go off into space now. Will you promise me?"

He stands up and takes both her paws in his. "There is no chance of me going into space and you know that. I'm just not the type they are looking for."

She dabs a tear from the corner of her eye with the tip of her apron. "I'm sorry to be such a ninny, but you are so like your father and you know what happened to him. Left me all alone to bring you up. Not a word or why-for!"

She dusts a wedding portrait of herself with his father, a broad-shouldered black rat with a long black beard, wearing a smart brown suit. Her tone turns gloomy. "Such a reckless fool, stowing away on that awful spaceship, never to be heard of again. Lost in space, probably dead for all I know." She sobs into the apron. "Oh what will become of you Uphrasia?! If I was to lose you I don't think my heart could stand it!"

Uphrasia puts his arm around her. "Mother don't carry on so. Even if there is the slimmest chance of a mission, I'll deliberately fail my astrophysics exam. Then they'll never send me on a mission."

She turns and hugs him, her voice back to a normal tone. "You're such a good boy. I'm not holding you back am I? I'd hate to think I was holding you back. But when you look at our family history, you'd be wise to avoid travel and adventure." She turns round and dusts off another portrait of a rat in a spacesuit, her voice goes back to the dark tone. "Great, great Uncle Ernie on the ill-fated Challenger mission. Burned to a crisp! Shocking!" The duster swipes another portrait of a rat in a captain's uniform. "Then there was my great, great grandfather Cyril, ran away to sea on the Titanic, sunk by an iceberg, frozen like a Popsicle!" She wraps her paws around her arms and shudders. "Chilling!" She flicks her duster at a small oval-framed picture of a sailor rat with a long white beard and a T-shirt with blue and white horizontal stripes. "And our ancestor Oswaldo Teach!" She turns with her eyes wider even than before and her paws clasped together. "Sailed aboard the Marie Celeste! Who knows what horrors befell that ghostly, doomed crew. Doomed they were. Doomed!!!"

He hugs her tightly and frowns over her shoulder. "OK, OK. I'll stay away from boats, ships, and spacecraft of any description. Don't fret so Mother!"

She lets out a deep sigh. "Thank goodness one of the Teach family has a tiny ounce of sense." There is a loud bump overhead and some soil drops through the root ceiling above them. "Those darned neighbours are at it again!" She picks up a broom and bangs on the ceiling. "Cut it out you noisy rascals!" She puts down the broom. "The whole neighbourhood has gone downhill ever since those foxes moved in. Turning over dustbins and bringing home litter!" She takes a shawl from the coat rack and throws it around her shoulders. "I'll walk you down the hill. No doubt you want to return to that awful school."

"There's no need Mother."

"Awe shush. Tell that young rascal Konrad I'll send you both some flapjack later on."

The forest has become dark as the group of foraging rats gather together in a semicircle before General Scrod. He stands in front of them with his back straight and his snout up. "Now then, show and tell everyone. Let me see what you have all foraged!" They produce nuts, berries, bugs and worms. Scout struggles with the very large wriggling beetle he caught. He holds its back legs as it fights and flails around. Finally, it breaks loose and runs off down the slope. Scrod raises one eyebrow and turns his snout down towards Konrad. "Konrad, what have you foraged for us today?" Konrad looks left and right then holds out a pawful of spindly twigs. Rose sniggers. Scrod clears his throat and she stands bolt upright to attention. Then Scrod steps over to Konrad and juts his chin down at him. "Twigs?!"

"Yes sir. Twigs sir." There is an uncomfortable silence. Konrad nibbles the end of a twig and raises both eyebrows innocently. "They're quite tasty, if there's nothing else around."

Scrod straightens up. "And where is Uphrasia, your foraging partner?!"

Konrad purses his lips. "Uphrasia, um, he had a sore ankle, so, he ah..."

"He absconded!"

"Yes sir, he ah, ab-, what you said, sir." Konrad looks at his feet.

Scrod clenches his paws and puts them on his hips. "Sounds to me like we have a couple of slackers in our unit." The other rats giggle. "Right!" Konrad is startled and straightens up. "Tomorrow, I want you and your lazy friend to report to me here after evening rations for foraging detention!"

Konrad bows his head. "Yes sir."

"Don't be late! The rest of you, well done. You've each earned ten merit points plus extra supper rations."

They all cheer and Rose punches the air. "Yes!"


Uphrasia enters the mess hall, collects his meal from the counter and takes his seat next to Konrad. There is a pile of twigs on the table in front of him. He nudges Konrad. "What's this?"

"I can explain. You see..."

"Hey, Uphrasia!" Roderick is standing on his chair waving a stick around. "Do you want some kindling for a starter?!"

Thompus shouts out "How about some branch water to wash it down with?!" Once again the whole mess hall breaks out in laughter.

Uphrasia's eyebrows point down in the middle. "Konrad! What've you done this time?!"

Konrad's bottom lip quivers. "I'm sorry. I tried to explain."

Roderick pipes up again, "What a pair of losers. Log on to the canteen website and see what twigs your interest!"

Thompus holds up a twig and waves it about. "Look at me! I like eating twigs!" All the rats in the mess hall roll around holding their tummies and laughing.

Roderick points the stick at Uphrasia. "You twig-eating morons won't even pass the exam tomorrow! Why are you even here at astro school? You will never graduate! Stick nibblers!"

Uphrasia gets up to leave as the elite rats gather round him. Thompus chuckles. "Have fun foraging with Scrod tomorrow night. Mind you don't eat the whole forest!"

Uphrasia slams his fist on the table. "I'll pass the exam and I'll show you all. You bunch of arrogant dimwits!"

He marches out of the hall, Roderick jeers. "You'll never pass, stick nibbler. Never!"

Uphrasia strides along the corridor, head down and teeth gritted as the laughter fades. Konrad trots up behind him. "Wait up! I'm sorry about all that buddy."

Uphrasia spins around, his face scrunched up with anger. "Don't buddy me! You keep messing things up for me. You're... holding me back!"

Konrad stands mouth open in shock. "Holding you back?"

"Just stay away from me!" He storms off.

"What do you mean I'm holding you back?"

Uphrasia stomps along the corridor and climbs up the dormitory ladder. He sits on his bed with his shoulders hunched holding a parcel with a note from his mother on it. It says "A little something for you and Konrad."

Uphrasia stares at the wall and contemplates. "Oh, cat poo! Poor old Konrad, he's not to blame for my situation. I'm just all out of options and it stinks!"

# Chapter 2

## FLY OF DESTINY

The small study room is clean and whitewashed. There are a few upturned ice-cream cartons and bookcases stuffed with textbooks. On a large blackboard on the wall someone has drawn a cartoon of a rat eating a twig. On the walls there are a few educational posters of spaceships, star systems and planets. Konrad sits alone hunched over a physics paper, frowning and scratching his head. A skinny finger arrives on the paper and points at part of an equation. "Gravity is why the light takes longer to reach us. It's bending the light. See?"

Konrad looks up to see Uphrasia standing over him. "Gravity. Thanks." He scribbles down the answer then looks back up at him. "Are we still pals then?"

"Sure. I'm sorry for getting mad at you. It's just those elite jerks really get under my fur."

"Yes, they were very rude. Very, very rude."

"I'm sick of being the butt of their jokes. I wish they'd all just disappear."

"You shouldn't say such things Uphrasia."

Uphrasia sits down opposite him looking gloomy. "I know."

He places the parcel on the table and Konrad sits bolt upright. "One of your mother's food parcels?"

"I felt so guilty when I saw it, I couldn't be mad at you anymore. Do the honours, pal."

Konrad rips off the layers of brown paper wrapping to reveal two large, perfectly round, oat flapjacks. Uphrasia grins. "Your favorites."

"Made with honey and just the right amount of sugar syrup. Thanks buddy!"

Uphrasia watches Konrad munching flapjack. "Konrad, I need some advice."

"Advice from me? Are you sure that's wise? I mean, look what happens when you leave me alone for five minutes. I think I must be the most unreliable rat in existence. If you take advice from me you're taking a huge gamble. That's all I'm saying."

"Don't worry about that. Look, I promised Mother I would fail the astrophysics exam tomorrow. She's worried about me going on a mission."

Konrad raises his eyebrows. "Well, like those Zucker rats said, you'll never pass the exam so you needn't worry."

"But I told those jerks I would pass, and to be honest, I've been studying pretty hard. I think I've got a shot."

"It certainly is a dilemma." He licks his lips and takes another huge bite.

Uphrasia holds out his arms. "What do I do?"

Konrad scratches his hip, takes another bite of flapjack and talks with his mouth full. "Simple. You pass the exam."

"But what about Mother? I can't lie to her."

Konrad waves a half-moon piece of flapjack around, his cheeks bulging. "Don't lie, just say nothing. Saying nothing is not lying, unless you say something, then it is."

Uphrasia scowls. "I sort of get what you mean." He gets up.

"Where are you going?"

"To study. I have a lot of swotting up to do."

"You'll pass, buddy. I know you will. Um, do you want this other piece of flapjack?"

Uphrasia smiles. "I don't want to get crumbs in the bed." He nods and leaves the room. Konrad raises his eyebrows twice and bites a big chunk off the other flapjack. He munches rapidly with his eyes closed, savoring every morsel.

The next morning, Uphrasia climbs out of his sleeping cubicle with a small computer tablet under his arm and an air of confidence about him. He slides down the ladder and marches along the corridor. He reaches a dilapidated wall with a big hole in the skirting board and slithers through to find Konrad waiting for him on the other side. They both join a line of other rats as they make their way along a wide metal pipe. Overhead pipes and conduits full of cables intertwine on the ceiling. A steady drip of water falls from the ceiling and vanishes into the darkness below making regular, loud plops. Konrad stares at the screen of his computer tablet and moves the controls with his thumbs. On the screen is his favourite game, Rat Maze. A rat on the screen hops about in a tunnel then presses a button on the wall and a large piece of cheese appears. The rat gobbles down the cheese. "What's a, val-er-dict-oryum?"

Uphrasia raises one eyebrow. "It's Valedictorian. It means I will be the key speaker at our graduation ceremony. I just have to trounce the astrophysics exam. Then, nothing can stand in my way. I'm going to be an officer Konrad. You'll be taking orders from me in the future."

Konrad scratches his chest. "Oh, poo, it won't be the same. We wouldn't be able to hang out together anymore."

"Yes, it's true. We will have to make some sacrifices in the name of progress dear boy. Are you playing that stupid Rat Maze again?"

Konrad keeps his eyes glued to the screen. "It's so addictive, I can't help myself."

"Turn it off, we're here."

Konrad switches off his tablet and slips it under his armpit as they reach an iron grate. Uphrasia slips through the bars into the corridor on the other side. Konrad squeezes through and gets stuck halfway. "Argh!" Uphrasia pulls him through by his arm. "Ta."

"Welcome."

They are joined by more rats, all holding their own computer tablets. Rose trots up, beaming a wide smile. "All ready for the exam then, Uphrasia?"

He rolls his eyes. "Fully revised, prepped and ready!"

She narrows her eyes. "Did you hear they changed the format this year?" He stops in his tracks.

"Format changed?!"

"Yes. The written test is followed by a practical test, construction of a molecule model from memory."

Uphrasia gulps. "A molecule model?!"

Konrad licks his lips from one side to the other with a loud slurp. "I love molecules, especially ones that make biscuits or pies." He licks his lips again.

Uphrasia slaps himself on the forehead. "But I can't remember all the molecules!" He stares at Konrad who stares back blankly, scratching his head. Uphrasia holds up his paws. "Any ideas?"

Konrad furrows his brow and thinks really hard, then furrows his brow again and rubs his chin. "Nope."

"Argh!"

The elite cadets arrive and Roderick halts them with his paw. "Hey look who it is. Uphrasia Teach, what are you doing here?"

Thompus swings his hips from side to side. "Stick nibblers sit at the back!"

Roderick nudges Uphrasia in the ribs. "Yeah, don't eat all the pencils!" They all giggle as they peel off into the exam room.

Furious, Uphrasia follows them in. "This joke is wearing pretty thin guys!"

A small, white albino rat walks along the corridor in the opposite direction. She has a shiny chrome plate on her head that covers her right eye and has a lens over it with small bright lights attached. There are a number of multi-coloured wires attached to the top of the plate that stick up in the air. She wears a white lab coat and a pair of headphones on her ears. Konrad stares at her and she pauses, looks at him with her one red eye while the lens on her right moves around, then points at him, focusing in. Then she hides her face behind her laptop and moves off along the corridor.

Konrad tugs on Rose's fur. "Who's the lab rat?"

"That's Nute, Professor Abler's granddaughter. She's some kind of genius, passed her astrophysics exam four months ago. Keeps herself to herself, super nerdy." She leans in close and whispers. "They live up in that tower above the sewage plant where they do experiments and all kinds of creepy science stuff."

Konrad's eyes widen. "Wow!"

Rose chuckles and ambles into the exam room. Konrad stands there in a daze and under his breath says, "Nute."

*Albino lab rats were bred for use by scientists and medical researchers. Many of the medicines we use today have been tested on such rats as these. Related to the brown rat, they are very intelligent.*

Uphrasia pops his head out of the room. "Konrad, exam!" Konrad snaps out of it and enters the exam room.

The bright, airy room has a high ceiling and sunlight streams in through tall windows along the whole length of one side. The students sit at rows of simple wooden desks chattering and fidgeting. Professor Abler is an aged albino lab rat wearing a white lab coat. He has a short, pointy white beard on the underside of his snout. His desk is a giant matchbox and he bangs on it with his fist making the matches rattle. His red eyes peer through his half-moon spectacles and his voice is croaky. "Now pay attention cadets. We have a special visitor today who would like to say a few words before the exam begins. Please welcome…" He clears his throat. "General Scrod!"

As Scrod enters all the students stand and applaud. Scrod fans his paw up and down. "All right, pipe down you lot. Pipe down!" They all sit down and settle. Scrod puffs up his chest. "I am here to tell you that we at Space Corps are looking for recruits for an intergalactic space mission to find a new home. We are somewhat overcrowded here on Earth and we all know the humans would prefer that we weren't here at all." Gasps and oohs. "I won't be joining the mission myself, as I am semi-retired." A big sigh from all the students. "We want the best of course, which is why only those who graduate from astro school will be accepted. I won't lie to you; this mission will be fraught with danger! It will be tough, but I know you will all do your best to be part of it. So good luck! That is all." He salutes, then marches out of the room. Scout salutes back and the other rats laugh at him.

Abler bangs on the desk again. "You may begin the exam. You have one hour to complete the written test! Switch on your tablets and open the file marked 'Astrophysics Exam'!" They all turn on their tablets and get started.

Konrad watches a fly buzz around his head following it with his snout going round and round in circles. It lands on the window and Konrad stares at it in a daze as it walks up and down. Uphrasia taps away at his tablet. The Zucker rats all work quickly, heads down, concentrating. Uphrasia looks at them and thinks, "I have to beat them. This could be my big break, I could actually get off this dead, miserable planet." Konrad flicks a wooden ruler on his desk and moves it to make a funny vibrating noise, sniggers, then does it again. Eventually the clock on the wall ticks from nine fifty to nine fifty-one. The Zucker rats begin to stand up one after the other; all except Thompus who continues to work. Rose stands up just after them. Uphrasia panics and types as fast as he can. Then he lets out a long sigh of relief, taps the send button and stands up just as the clock strikes ten.

Abler looks at his watch. "Right, that's time. E-mail me your files. If you have not finished, email them anyway! We will have a fifteen-minute break, then we will move on to the next test: construction of a molecule!" Thompus looks around the room. It seems everyone except for him has finished the exam. He taps send on his tablet and follows the others out of the room.

Uphrasia fills a paper cup from a dripping pipe and takes a drink. Konrad arrives, fills his cup and asks. "How did you get on with the test?"

"I think I nailed it. Hard to tell, those multiple choice questions were really tricky."

"What if you pass, because, clearly, I won't?"

"What do you mean?"

"Well, you will go on a mission and I will have to stay here. We may never see each other again."

Uphrasia takes a gulp of water and frowns. "I haven't thought that far ahead buddy. Maybe they will let me have an assistant."

Konrad looks forlorn, knowing the truth in his mind. "I don't think they would allow that. He'll go into space and I'll be left behind."

Uphrasia pats him on the shoulder. "Something will present itself. It always does. We always stick together. Through thick and thin."

Konrad looks up at him and smiles. "We do don't we? On flapjack days and also on days when there is no flapjack. Through thick and thin."

"Yep! Through thick and thin. Come on, let's get this rotten exam over with."

Back in the exam room all the rats queue up in a line as Abler gives each one a tray filled with red, white and blue balls on small wooden sticks. They all return to their desks. Konrad makes a huge yawn and stares out of the window. Abler clears his throat. "I want you all to construct a carbohydrate molecule from memory. You have twenty minutes. Begin now!"

Konrad sits up straight. "Carbohydrate!" His tummy rumbles and he rubs it. "Oh... Twenty minutes is such a long time to wait for your next installment of food." He looks around the room then over at Abler. Then he reaches under his desk and takes out a small parcel of paper and unwraps a small chunk of flapjack. He nibbles it, keeping an eye on Abler.

Rose and Uphrasia get to work. Uphrasia's tongue hangs out of the side of his mouth. "Carbohydrate – carbohydrate?" He sorts out the shapes on his tray and scratches the tuft of hair on his head. "Sugar's a carbohydrate, right?"

Konrad balances a small white ball on his nose, then he puts one in his mouth and rolls it around his cheeks, then swallows it with a loud gulp. "Oops!" Then he plays with two rat dolls he has constructed out of the molecule kit, moving them as if in slow

33

motion. "Hey, Uphrasia, let's go to space, OK Konrad! Wee…"

Uphrasia has nearly completed his molecule, but the elite rats are way ahead and they all stand up; all except Thompus. Rose stands up a moment later. Abler looks up at the clock and adjusts his spectacles. "Well done. You are the first to finish! I think we have found our senior science graduates."

Konrad is fast asleep with his head in the tray, snoring. As he breathes in a large red ball rolls up and sticks to his left nostril and then rolls back again as he snores out. Uphrasia desperately tries to complete his molecule, but the clock is getting closer and closer to twenty past ten. He tugs on a ball that is stuck in the wrong place. It won't budge. He yanks on it hard and the whole molecule falls apart. He looks at the clock, nineteen minutes past. Uphrasia tries to reconstruct the molecule. The clock hits twenty past. Abler stands up. "Right, cadets, your time is up. Put down your molecule and leave the exam room."

Uphrasia scrunches up his face. "No, it can't be!" In a tantrum he picks up a large red ball and throws it hard at the floor. It bounces up, hits a wall, ricochets off the ceiling and out of an open window. The ball rolls along the window ledge, falls into the gutter, runs along it, drops down into a drain pipe and spirals down. It pops out at the bottom, bounces off a level concrete platform and rises back up into the air. Then it lands on a square metal fan housing and rolls gently into a rusty hole in the middle. Inside a huge metal fan spins rapidly and the ball gets sucked into the whirling blades. It fires out smashing a hole in the protective wire mesh grille and zooms downwards.

The school Principal, an ancient Zucker rat, stands in an open courtyard talking to a mixed group of young, keen-looking rats. "Now, if you study hard you may all graduate. But you must study very hard." The ball darts through the air down towards the Principal and it slams onto the top of his head. His body goes rigid and he falls sideways onto the ground.

In a long, tall and brightly lit corridor Konrad sits on a tiny bench humming quietly to himself and swinging his legs as he watches that fly buzzing round his head again. Next to him, neatly cut out in the skirting board, is a wooden door with a sign over which reads "PRINCIPAL'S OFFICE". An angry voice shouts from within "Now get out of my sight. Insolent young rat! I've never seen the like! Never!"

The door opens and Uphrasia exits with his head bowed, looking dejected. The fly zips inside just as he closes the door.

Konrad hops down and blinks at him. "How did it go?"

"He didn't suspend me, but as I failed to complete the exam I won't make the grade. I'll be a total laughing stock now and those Zucker rats will make my life a misery."

Konrad smiles. "Well, we're used to that. Anyway, you'll climb up through the ranks in no time. Let's go to lunch, I'm starving."

"Konrad! How can you think of food? Don't you get it? My life is over!"

"Every cloud has a silver lining."

"No chance of a mission!"

"Travel is overrated."

"I'll have to leave Astro School, no more of Mum's food parcels!"

Konrad's eyes bulge. "This is a disaster! We have to do something!"

The Principal sits at his huge desk sporting a large, red, bald bump between his tufty ears. He holds two wooden ink stamps, one in each paw. He slams a stamp on the first of a huge pile of the rats' school records and it leaves the word "FAILED!" in bright red letters. He then places the record in an out tray. At the top of the record is a photograph of Thompus. The fly buzzes around the Principal's head. He flaps his arms around and the fly lands on Konrad's school record. Slam! He squashes the fly flat! The Principal lifts up the stamp to reveal the word PASSED. He grins a wicked grin. "Ha, got you, filthy germ-carrying swine!" He picks up Konrad's record, looks at it and scratches his head and his finger touches the sore, throbbing bump in the middle of his forehead. "Ouch," he winces. Then he shrugs his shoulders and tosses Konrad's record into the out tray.

The maggot farm is an extremely smelly place; not surprising considering it is inside a sewage plant. But this sour and rank stink is enough to turn any stomach, apart from a rat's that is. It's damp and dingy, with rows of worktops covered with rotting vegetation, mouldy sausages and rancid fish heads in trays of writhing maggots. Rose enters through a door and tips a bucket of food waste onto one of the maggot trays. Uphrasia and Konrad are halfway down the room wearing white waterproof suits. They stroll along between the maggot beds with water tanks on their backs with pipes leading to spray guns they hold in their paws. Every now and then they spray a jet of water over the maggots. "My feet are cold," Konrad complains. "Plus I don't like eating maggots. Why are they even on the menu?"

Uphrasia sprays a tray of maggots. "Konrad. You know there are food shortages. And I told you a hundred times to wear your boots."

Up at the far end Nute enters wearing her white lab coat. She adjusts the focus of her lens with her paw and she sees a grid on the internal screen and a maggot comes into focus. She inserts a syringe into the maggot and draws out some green slime. Then she empties the syringe into a test tube and seals it with a cork. She holds it up and her lens' motor whirs, moving back and forth to focus on the tube. Konrad stares at her. Rose's voice whispering in his ear startles him, "More hideous experiments!"

Konrad's eyes widen and Rose grins. "You like her don't you?" Konrad shuffles his paws and points his toes point together. "Would you like to meet her?"

Uphrasia chuckles. "Konrad on a date, ha, ha, what a laugh. Can you imagine?"

Konrad looks up at Rose with his bright beady eyes. "Yes! I would like to meet her, as a matter of fact." He rocks his paws from side to side.

Rose gives Uphrasia a sly look. "Do you know the manure mound at the edge of the sewage plant?"

Uphrasia gives the maggots a dousing with his spray gun and says nonchalantly. "I am aware of the place."

"Great, it's a date. We'll meet you both there after evening rations." She walks towards the exit.

Uphrasia has to think fast. "We can't. We have foraging detention!"

"OK, after you get back then!" She exits with Nute, closing the door before he can respond.

"What just happened there?! Did I just get conned into a date with that soppy, fancy rat?"

Konrad grins from ear to ear. "Oh come on, it'll be fun. Besides, I need your back up. I don't know how to talk to girls."

"And you suppose I do?"

Konrad raises his eyebrows in the middle, putting on his best sad face. It always works. Uphrasia looks up to the ceiling and sighs. "OK, OK, we'll go. Just stop looking like a constipated mime artist."

Konrad jumps up and claps his paws together. "Yes!"


The stubby tower that sits on top of the sewage plant is lit from within by a dim light that glows through the boards and sooty windows. Inside there is clutter everywhere. The shelves are stuffed with bottles of chemicals and glass jars filled with dead insects, invertebrates and reptiles floating in green formaldehyde liquid. There are rows and rows of books and files. Machines and electronic gadgets whir and buzz on the long counters and chemicals in round glass bottles bubble over gas burners, as does a clear glass beaker with two eggs boiling in it. A large blue plastic box on wheels is filled with old electronic gadgets, laptops, tablets, mobile phones and lots of other discarded human things the rats have collected from the city dump. They are so resourceful that there is not much they cannot repair or reuse. In many cases they even improve things.

Professor Abler is bent over a counter with his head inside a metal box full of wires and circuits. The door intercom makes a loud buzz and he straightens up bumping his head inside the box. "Ouch!" He pulls out his head, rubbing it. "Fiddlesticks!" He walks over to the entrance door and looks at a small screen on the intercom. Uphrasia's face looks back at him. Abler presses a switch and the entrance door opens.

"You wanted to see me, Professor?"

"Yes, yes, come in young rat, come in."

Uphrasia enters, looking all around at the contraptions and machines. A marble maze catches his eye. He watches as a marble rolls along a slot, falls down a steep shoot and lands on a conveyer belt. Then it is carried back up to the top where it starts its journey all over again. Abler looks him up and down through his spectacles. "Uphrasia Teach, I have been watching your progress with some interest over these past few years."

"You have, sir?"

Abler opens a tall filing cabinet and rummages around. "I have. Your test results are very good, considering."

"Considering I'm a common sewer rat?"

Abler pulls his head out of the cabinet and frowns over his half-moon spectacles. "Considering your academic background and the fact that your father left home when you were a young kit. You've done fairly well, but you could do a lot better. Could you not?"

"Well I, ah..."

His head goes back into the cabinet. "Now where is it? Aha!" He pops back out holding a small black box. "I'd like to think I can trust you, young rat?"

The red eyes stare at him so intently that Uphrasia feels uncomfortable.

"You can sir, of course."

Abler gives him the box. "Good. Ever since Nute's parents died in that tragic road-kill incident I've had the troubling responsibility of watching over her. I worry about her, you see. She's…" He looks up at the ceiling. "She's an unusual rat. This radio locator will work within a certain distance. At least, I think it will. She has a tracker implanted under her fur, the type humans invented to locate their lost pets." He gives Uphrasia five tiny, glowing, glass tubes. "These power cells have a long life but use them wisely." He looks around the room and sighs. "All these things the humans threw away. What good they could have done with them instead of destroying everything in their path. Such a race, such pointless waste of potential." Abler places one paw on Uphrasia's shoulder and guides him towards the exit. "I want you to take good care of this device and keep an eye on Nute for me." He breathes in and lets out a sigh. "You see, I won't be around for a lot longer. I'd like to think she will have some friends she can rely upon, when I'm gone."

Uphrasia frowns and tries to give back the box. "Sir, I don't think I'm qualified. I failed my astrophysics exam."

"Don't worry about that. I have had a word with the Principal, and he has come around to my way of thinking. Once he calmed down. You have made the grade. You are no longer a Space Corps cadet." He salutes. "Private Teach!"

Uphrasia's eyes widen and he salutes. "Yes sir! Thank you sir!"

"You have just squeezed through the keyhole. But you will have to work twice as hard from now on. Don't let me down after I have stuck my neck out for you."

"I won't sir!"

"You know your father had a quality like no other rat I have ever met. You have great potential, Uphrasia Teach. You just need to unlock it."

Uphrasia stares at the box then up at Abler. "You knew my father?"

"Yes I knew Edward very well. He would be proud to see how you've grown. I know you must miss him very much."

"He never said goodbye. Do you know where he went?"

"Nobody knows that but Edward my boy. He had an adventurous heart, could never settle in one place for long."

"Look where adventure has gotten my family? All of my ancestors met with a horrible end! I promised Mother I would never go on a mission."

"Don't you ever feel like you were destined for something greater?"

"Destined?"

"It's in all of us Uphrasia. It's why we have spread all over this planet so successfully. We have a deep yearning for adventure and exploration. It's in our genes.

Uphrasia looks very solemn. "Do you suppose he's still alive, my father?"

"Edward was, is, a most resourceful and brave rat. I am sure whatever challenges he met, he would have overcome. I remember he once took on a cat and you can guess who came out on top. Who knows, one day you may bump into him again."

"It's a big universe."

Abler nods. "Yes, it is. Now will you do as I ask? Keep an eye on Nute for me?"

"Well, I suppose."

"Good chap, now off you go." He ushers him out through the exit and closes the door before he can change his mind. Abler turns around looking very serious. "Well Edward, I kept my promise." He opens a drawer and takes out an envelope addressed to Uphrasia Teach. He takes out a letter and reads it. At the bottom are the words: "With love from your father." He folds it up and puts it in his lab-coat pocket. "I'll give it to him when the time is right. Yes. When the time is right."

# Chapter 3
## 1000 VOLTS

A cold wind rushes through the forest, rustling the long grass and swirling tiny snowflakes around. A fox trots through the trees then stops abruptly and listens, staring intently into the distance; careful, cautious, before moving on, sniffing the ground looking for a scent and then vanishing into the dark undergrowth.

General Scrod stands in a clearing next to a small fire with his arms folded and snout up high. Uphrasia and Konrad walk up to him wearing rucksacks sporting a shiny new Space Corps logo on their backs. They look at each other then back up at Scrod who does not move his head. "The jungle is a hazardous environment!" He looks down, narrowing his eyes. "One small error and it's all over for you!" He opens his own rucksack, takes out two small pen-knives and gives them one each.

Konrad opens his and feels the blade edge. "Wow cool!"

"Against all the odds you have both graduated today." He widens his eyes. "When I look at you young chaps I'm reminded of myself in my youth." He sits down on the ground and they follow suit. "You see, I was just like you, a simple young rat trying to make my way in life. No one expected me to amount to anything, yet look at me now, a decorated general! Nothing is impossible if you try very hard!"

Uphrasia frowns. "How did you do it sir? How did you overcome your humble beginnings?"

"I had to train more and study harder than any other rat. That's what it all boils down to lad, hard work!" They stare at him impressed. "Things were very different back then, we had harsher times with the great freeze and a serious lack of food. So we had to fight to survive. It was a struggle but we all made it through. Now off you go and find me something we can actually eat this time. You have two hours before darkness falls. Move out!"

They both march off and Scrod shouts after them. "Keep a look out for owls, foxes, badgers, bats, stoats, weasels, mink and buzzards." Scrod's voice fades as they move away up a steep slope. "Grass snakes, vipers, adders, dogs, cats, ferrets, funnel-web spiders, black widow spiders, oh and the false widow spider, they are very tricky to spot!"

They walk through the undergrowth looking left and right, straining their ears to listen for predators. As they crawl through a thick holly bush there is the sound of a twig cracking! They freeze on the spot not moving a muscle. The fox creeps past the bush sniffing the air close to them. The icy wind is blowing in their favour so she does not pick up their scent. She moves past the bush then trots away up the icy path. They both let out a deep breath then creep up to the edge

46

of the bush and peep out. All is clear so they dart across the path. They reach the edge of the forest to see the vast vista of Grumthorpe lit up in the failing dusky light. Konrad stares at the city, the bright glittering lights reflected in his shiny black eyes. "Why do the humans hate us so much?"

"They're afraid of us, now that we're smart."

"Because of Gorgonzola the Great?"

Uphrasia nods. "Because of Gorgonzola the Great."

Konrad looks around his feet. "Suppose we better find something for General Scrod then."

Uphrasia turns up one side of his mouth and winks a sly wink. "I don't think so."

"Not again. You're not leaving me alone to face Scrod!"

"No of course not. However, I just might know a short cut to some great foraging. Although it might be a tad risky."

Konrad looks puzzled. "Risky. How risky?"

A tall brick wall rises up before them and on the wire fence above a rusty sign warns "DANGER ELECTRIC FENCE 1000 VOLTS!" Uphrasia starts to climb up the wall and Konrad clasps his paws together in a panic. "But this is a human place, forbidden!"

Uphrasia pauses and cranes his head around. "Come on, I want to show you something!"

"OK but I am submitting a formal protest right now, OK?" Konrad follows him up to the top of the wall and they look through the wire fence at a gigantic flood-lit garden filled with neat lines of crops. Carrots, cabbages, onions, turnips and beetroot sit on the soft brown soil and tall sweetcorn waves in the breeze. Giant pumpkins and climbing cucumbers weave around the fence and neatly pruned fruit trees stand against the far wall. At the back of the garden is a long greenhouse containing winter salads, tomatoes and luscious fat watermelons. Along the centre of the garden are rows of purple sprouting broccoli, cauliflowers and broad beans.

Uphrasia grabs the fence with both paws and shakes violently. "Ah!!!"

Konrad's hair stands on end. "Uphrasia!"

Uphrasia lets go and laughs, holding his belly.

Konrad looks very cross. "You, swine! That wasn't funny!"

"Oh boy, I really had you that time! Ha! Your face!"

Konrad rolls his eyes impatiently. "What is this place?"

"It's where the humans grow their food, there's bound to be a ton of slugs here."

"Are you sure it's safe."

"Nope. Come on!"

They look left and right, then climb up the fence over the top and down the other side, dropping down onto the ground. Konrad whispers as they creep along the line of carrots. "How do you know about this?"

"My father used to come here. He'd bring us food back. Kept us alive during the long winters."

"It's warm here."

"The lights keep the crops growing all year round."

"We should tell everyone. They should all know about this food source. Just think, no more crispy fried worms." Konrad stops in his tracks, his eyes wide. "No more slug rationing!"

Uphrasia raises his paws, palms down. "No! You know the law. If we admit we came here..."

"We'd be punished for treason, banished, outcasts! They would torture us first to get the truth, then the iron maiden, the rack, hung drawn and quartered!"

"Well, they would certainly be very cross with us. Remember what you said? How saying nothing is not lying? If we just keep this between ourselves..."

"Then we're not lying." Konrad looks around the garden and Uphrasia heads off, leaving Konrad talking to himself staring up at a tall sweetcorn. "But that was just my advice. I mean, I didn't expect you to take any notice. I was just trying to help in a bad situation. I wouldn't listen to anything I say, after all look at the humongous catastrophes I get us into if left on my own. You have to admit I..." He looks down realising he's alone, looks left, then right and races off. "Uphrasia wait for me!"

Konrad wanders along a line of runner beans, grabbing armfuls of fat, ripe beans. He pulls up a carrot and then an onion. He stops suddenly, staring down into a ditch. Then he drops all he is carrying and his bottom jaw drops.

Uphrasia appears behind him. "What is it?"

Konrad stares at him with a look of amazement and in a low, husky voice says, "It's the slug motherlode!"

At the bottom of the ditch burried in the ground is a large plastic bowl containing twelve fat slugs floating in a pool of brown beer. They both climb down and poke their heads into the bowl and take a sip of beer. Konrad licks his lips. "Yummy! Let's take some back to Scrod."

Uphrasia stands up straight and folds his arms and frowns. "No!"

"Huh?"

Uphrasia grins. "Let's take all of them!"

"Now you're talking!"

They hobble along through the garden carrying the bowl between them. Uphrasia spots a mangy, skinny, tabby cat lying on a compost bin bathing in the heat of the flood lights. "Konrad, a cat, keep low." He whispers and they both duck down and creep past the compost bin. The cat rolls on its back, stretches and yawns, then curls up again and continues to doze. Konrad sweats and struggles to keep a grip on the bowl. The cat opens its eyes, scowls and sniffs twice.

There is something familiar on the air. It stretches its legs then jumps down onto the ground. Uphrasia and Konrad carry the heavy load up to the edge of a deep winding brook that runs the full length of the garden and exits under a tall wire fence. They pause for a rest. Konrad pokes his nose into the bowl and takes a long sniff. "Core, smells pretty boozy. Remember that time we drank that miniature bottle of whisky? What a night that was!"

Uphrasia stares up at something behind Konrad. "Uh hum."

"Boy we had rotten hangovers the next morning!"

"Uh hum!"

"You got your head stuck in that toilet roll tube, what a giggle! How we laughed at you."

"Uh hum!!"

Konrad stops talking and frowns. "The cat's behind me, isn't it?"

Uphrasia talks without moving his lips, "Don't make any sudden moves."

The cat's nose moves right up to Konrad's left ear and sniffs. Konrad swallows and makes a loud gulp. The cat hisses!

"When I shout 'now', leap into the stream, and keep hold of the bowl," Uphrasia whispers. Then he leans down very slowly and picks up a stone. Using his thumb and forefinger he flicks it into a line of runner beans where it clatters off the bamboo canes. The cat's head darts left towards the sound. "Now!" They both leap off the bank and splash into the water holding tightly onto the bowl. The cat swipes a claw after Konrad just missing his head, then loses its balance and slides down the river bank after him. It claws at the roots and mud then falls into the stream with a big splash.

Konrad goes under the water then pops back up. Choking and spluttering, he grabs the edge of the bowl and hangs on. The cat meows and claws, thrashing right behind him. "It's swimming after me!"

"Cats can't swim!"

"Then it's drowning after me! Help!"

The cat catches Konrad's tail, clamping its sharp teeth onto the end of it. "Ouch!" Konrad wails. The cat paddles desperately with its paws tugging at Konrad's tail. They duck under the water as they pass beneath the fence, the bowl just scraping under the wire. The cat hits the fence and clings on, letting out a low angry growl! Konrad stops with a jolt and lets go of the bowl and Uphrasia floats away. The cat pulls hard on his tail. "Ouch! Uphrasia I'm done for!" he shouts as he is slowly dragged back towards the cat's jaws. The cat pulls hard and tugs and tugs and Konrad's tail stretches. Then there is a loud snap! The end of Konrad's tail breaks off and he floats off downstream. Konrad looks back over his shoulder at the soaking moggy holding on to the fence with the little tail tip still in its teeth. "Phew!" The cat scowls at him then chews the tail and swallows. Konrad swims over to a low sandy shore where Uphrasia is waiting. They drag the bowl out of the stream and shake the water off their fur.

"Are you OK?"

Konrad looks at the sore end of his tail, revealing raw, red flesh and bone. "I guess so." He flops onto his back, puffing. "Wow! That was too close for comfort!"

"And to think my father foraged here every week! Come on, let's get back to camp and dry off by the fire."

Konrad scrambles to his feet and picks up his side of the bowl. "That cat must have got plenty of exercise."

# Chapter 4

# EXTERMINATION

In her cosy little den, Mother opens her oven which is a large catering tin can with a door that her husband Edward made for her. She takes out a small tray of steaming flapjacks and places them on a cooling rack. When they are cool she wraps them up in brown paper. "That school will starve those poor boys with their meagre rations." She writes a short message for Uphrasia on the paper and squeezes herself out through the entrance tunnel. She pops out of the hole in the curb just as the red setting sun dips below the horizon. Then she hums cheerfully as she heads down the steep hill towards the sewage plant.

In his cubicle Thompus packs his belongings into his small rucksack. He takes a last look at his school report pinned on the wall with the word "FAILED" stamped on it and lets out a sigh. He walks out through the mess hall past the other rats who are busy chatting, eating and celebrating their success. Not even the other Zucker rats pay him any attention as he walks out through the exit door.

A large grey truck drives through the tall gates of the sewage plant, the headlights making a bright arc across the flat roof. On the side of the van is a picture of a shocked rat with a bolt of lightning through its chest, surrounded by a circle of bright red words, "PEST EXTERMINATORS!" Two men wearing clean white protective coveralls, breathing masks and head torches get out. They open a side door, pull out two long hoses and drag them to a row of ten small, vertical air vents poking out of the flat roof of the plant. In the light of the van headlights one of the men seals eight of the vents with sticky tape while the other attaches the hoses to the two remaining. Then he opens the doors at the back of the van to reveal two large gas tanks marked "POISON!" over a skull and cross bones! He pulls down a metal lever and the pipes begin to hiss.

The feint yellow glow of Scrod's campfire lights up the clearing. Uphrasia and Konrad struggle down the slope towards it trying to keep the heavy bowl level. Scrod sits beside the fire holding a stick with a dried wrinkly worm on the end of it. He turns it slowly over the flames then nibbles the end of the worm and makes a gagging face. "Yuck!" They plonk the bowl on the ground and flop down beside the warm fire rubbing their paws and holding them up to the flames. Scrod gets up and peers into the bowl then scratches his head. "I've never seen such plump slugs!" He pops the slug into his mouth, chews and swallows it. He raises his eyebrows and licks his lips. "India Pale Ale if I'm not mistaken. We should eat them before they spoil. After all it's going to be a long night."

Konrad panics. "Long night? Aren't we going back now?"

"No, tonight we sleep under the stars." He burps, looking up at the first star twinkling in the grey sky. "Get the whole wilderness experience."

Konrad whispers behind his paw. "Uphrasia, what about our dates?"

Uphrasia puts up his paw. "General, sir, couldn't we take the slugs back to share with the others?"

"You're forgetting the Rat Way! If we share these slugs, we would be turning our backs on our own nature. You wouldn't want that now, would you?"

Uphrasia frowns. "Uh, no sir, I guess not."


Rose and Nute sit side by side on a huge mound of steaming manure. They stare at the view of Grumthorpe, now fully lit with the lights of the traffic streaking over and under the motorways. Gaudy signs flash with neon and plumes of grey smoke rise from the factory chimneys and vanish into the darkened sky. Nute wrinkles her forehead and looks up at Rose. "Where do you suppose they are?"

Rose shakes her head. "They probably got held up. I bet they are sprucing themselves up right now, you know, so they look their best."

"Do you think he'll like me?"

"Why wouldn't he?"

Nute strokes one of the wires on her head. "They frighten people away."

"Let me tell you, he likes you. He told me so."

The corner of Nute's mouth turns up slightly. "Really?"

Rose nods.

Nute looks back at the sparkling lights of the city. "I suppose we could wait a little longer then. Just so they have time to look their best." They sit silhouetted against the glittering city. "I had that dream again last night. I feel in my wires that something terrible will befall us."

Rose looks at her with narrowed eyes. She knows that when Nute gets a bad feeling about something she is generally right. "What did you dream?"

Nute shakes her head and looks up at the moon. "I saw horror, dead faces floating on a cloud among the stars." Rose puts her arm around Nute's shoulder and Nute pulls her knees up and wraps her paws around them. "We can't live here. I know we have to go but no one will believe me."

"What about your grandfather, Professor Abler?"

"He doesn't hold with my visions, he's all about logic. If there is no evidence to prove it, then it's not real."

"I must admit your dream frightens me."

"You know I'm never wrong."

"But, where would we go? We are surrounded by wilderness and we can't live in Grumthorpe City. It's overpopulated with cats. Not forgetting the humans hate us."

Nute stares up at the stars. "Up there, that's where we have to go."

Rose looks up at the bright moon. "Up there?"

"You know they are planning a mission, to the stars. We have to be on that mission Rose. We just have to."

"So many rats have made the grade, we are way down the pecking order."

"Still, we must be on that spaceship"

Rose frowns. "You're talking about stowing away."

"Isn't that exactly what we are meant to do? We are rats after all."

"We don't have the equipment or the spacesuits."

"Let me see to that. Will you go with me if we are not selected Rose?"

Rose looks at the city and purses her lips. "I can't see why not. There's not a lot left for us here."

Nute nuzzles her head into Rose' side.


The fire in the camp is now blazing as heavy snowflakes fall and settle on the ground all around them. Scrod, Uphrasia and Konrad lie on their backs, bellies bulging. Konrad lets out a long, low burp.

"Argh! I feel dizzy." A snowflake lands on his nose; he looks at it, cross eyed, as it melts.

Uphrasia is uncommonly cheerful. "I feel great! How about a song?"

Scrod burps. "Good idea!" He furrows his brow. "I don't know any songs. Songs never really came up in military training."

Konrad sits bolt upright. "I know the perfect song! Burp!"

Uphrasia counts to four and Konrad starts to sing in a squeaky tone.

*"It's tough at the bottom of the food chain."*

Uphrasia joins in slightly out of tune.

*"When every single day is do or die,*
 *and whenever you look up,*
 *all you see is someone's butt,*
 *crapping down on you from on high!"*

Scrod joins in with some of the words and they sing at the top of their voices.

*"Yes it's tough at the bottom of the food chain, when no one seems to care or wonder why. You're bound to stink a bit, when you're swimming round in shoo-ooh-oo-*

*wage. The scorn of every single passer-by!"*

Scrod chuckles. "That's a fine song. Where did you learn it?"

The smile disappears from Uphrasia's face and he stares into the dancing flames. "Father used to sing it to me." They settle down next to the fire and curl up to go to sleep. Scrod places a few more branches on the fire then lays down looking into the flames and closes his eyes.

Dawn breaks and red sunlight filters through the barren trees now with a layer of snow on their branches. The three awake, stretching and yawning. Scrod holds his head. "Oh my brain hurts." He rubs his face with some of the snow that covers the forest floor. They cover up the burnt patch of the fire with dirt, then Scrod leads them back along the icy path in single file.

Konrad's teeth chatter and he turns up the collar of his tunic. "My it's gotten cold quickly."

Uphrasia stamps his feet and rubs his paws together. "It's going to be a harsh winter."

"I hear it's very cold in space."

"It is. Very, very cold. We are better off here if you ask me."

The sewage plant is unusually quiet as they march in through the gate, not noticing the fresh tire tracks in the snow under their feet. Scrod enters the mess hall first and freezes, staring aghast at a horrible sight. "Dear Gorgonzola preserve us!" The other two enter and stand next to him, their mouths open. Konrad hides his face in his paws. The mess hall is full of dead rats. The elite Zucker rats are piled up on one of the long tables. Scrod lifts one of their heads. It's Roderick, his face contorted, his mouth open wide. Scrod lets out a deep sigh. "I've seen this before. Gassed! All dead. Those inhuman humans!" He gently lowers Roderick's head.

Professor Abler, Rose and Nute enter the room. Rose holds Nute by the paw, fresh tears glisten on their furry cheeks. "Um, Uphrasia." Rose's voice breaks up, she covers her mouth and shakes her head.

Professor Abler takes hold of Uphrasia by the arm. "You'd better come with me young fellow." Abler puts his grey paw on Uphrasia's shoulder, turns him around and guides him out of the room.

In the long dormitory corridor, the floor is littered with more dead rats. Some hang out of their sleeping boxes, some lie on the floor holding onto each other. All wear the same desperate expression. On the floor at Uphrasia's feet, still clutching the food parcel, is Mother. He drops to his knees and lifts up her limp paw and whispers, "Mother."

Mother stirs and her voice is faint and raspy, "Is that you, my boy?"

He cradles her in his arms. "Yes, it's me Mother."

"I was wrong, it's not safe here my love. Follow your dreams." With that she lets out a long breath of green gas and closes her eyes. Uphrasia leans over her and weeps.

Abler kneels beside him and pats him on the back. "So tragic. There, there, my boy. There, there."

Uphrasia looks up, face creased with rage. "Those rotten humans, I hate them, I hate them!" He lowers his head and sobs. "I hate them."


All the surviving rats are gathered on the banks of a wide river. Around a hundred tiny rafts are lined up with at least one dead rat on each, some with two, many with three. Uphrasia places a lit candle next to his mother's body. Then he pushes the tiny craft out onto the water. The other rats push their loved ones out into the current. Thompus heaves his raft into the water, then steps back and wipes his nose and sniffs, watching Roderick's body float away. A line of tiny lights drift towards a huge waterfall that drops a hundred feet and thunders into a foaming rapid. Mother's raft reaches the edge and tips over. The candle goes out as the raft is swallowed by falling white water. Nute watches misty eyed, the vision from her dream now a reality as the clouds reflect in the water and the faces of her comrades float by illuminated by tiny candles. Scrod gathers the survivors near the river bank. "A solemn day. Many friends lost and barely any elite cadets left for our mission. Yet the mission must proceed. We have no choice now. For reasons beyond our understanding we have been spared this horrible fate. But clearly we can't stay here anymore. I will have to lead the mission myself!"

He looks at Rose. "Will you lead a team Rose?" She nods in silence. He turns to Professor Abler and Nute. "Our science team bore heavy losses. Will you step up?" Then he turns his attention to the new recruits. "Uphrasia and Konrad, we will need smart young rats on this mission." Uphrasia stares, a cold glazed stare, unable to form words in his mouth.

Konrad takes a step forward. "We will do our duty General." He squeezes Uphrasia's arm. "Won't we, pal?" Uphrasia nods.

"It's decided then, the rest of our survivors will take on the vacated roles. We must gather equipment and supplies. May Gorgonzola grant us all a safe passage." He straightens up and puffs out his chest. "What are we?!"

They all mumble together, "Survivors."

His voice is deep and booming. "What are we?!!"

They all shout, "Survivors!!"

"That's right! Because we survive!"

The rats race about the sewage plant rooms and corridors collecting equipment and supplies. Scout leads a group of ten scruffy misfits marching in line two by two, all out of time, wearing ill-fitting uniforms. All the smaller and youngest rats of the colony who were sleeping safely at home.

Nute and Professor Abler pack electronic gadgets into a large kit bag. Abler checks off a list in his paw. "Toxin tester, atmosphere analyser, radiation Geiger counter, water purifying tablets." He strokes his beard. "What am I missing?" He looks at Nute and she smiles.

"Spacesuits!"

"Ah of course we wouldn't get far without our spacesuits." He pockets his list, places his paws on his hips and smiles. "Well, you got the mission you wanted young lady. I hope you are prepared for what is to come."

"I am Grandpappy!"

On the walls of a locker room hang many spacesuits. On the shelves above, rows of shiny new space helmets. Konrad steps into a spacesuit, pulls it up over his hips and pushes his arms in. Then he tries to zip up the front. The zipper gets stuck halfway up his belly. "This one's no good, it's far too small for me."

Uphrasia zips his own suit up to his neck. "It's the largest one we could find." He puts his foot on Konrad's tummy, pushes down hard as Konrad pulls on the zip and it slides up. Konrad's tummy bulges. "Phew! No room for extra rations in here."

"They all seem to be Zucker rat sizes. Try not to bend over or it may rip. We'll get it adjusted on the ship."

Konrad frowns and purses his lips. "I'm scared Uphrasia."

"Don't worry, old pal. We'll be OK. Just follow the Rat Way and nothing bad will happen. Just think, at least we are still together."

"Yes, I suppose."

"We'll watch each other's back. Agreed?"

Konrad smiles. "Agreed."

Scrod enters. "Get a move on you two. Everyone else has already left!"

Konrad looks up at him with his little beady round eyes. "I had a little trouble with my suit, sir."

"So I see. Well, hurry up and get out of it. We have a long journey ahead and you can't march in that outfit." He grunts and marches out. They take down their helmets, hold them under their arms and stand looking each other up and down.

"Well this is it, old friend. No turning back now. We are going into outer space to face the unknown, adventure and danger." Uphrasia grins.

"I'm going to miss my cosy cubicle."

"We'll have more room in our new quarters and best of all we get to share."

"Do you think they have slugs in space?"

"Slugs are everywhere pal. Slugs are everywhere!"

# Chapter 5
## EXODUS

Rats don't mourn for long. With such short lives, death is a familiar thing to them. Yet the pain Uphrasia felt when his mother died still burns, although buried deep down somewhere inside. Through urgent necessity he pulled himself out of his slump and forged forward with all the other rats. After all, they had all lost someone close to them, they were all in this together. So he took a deep breath and joined them in the brave march towards the future, whatever that might be.

For some time the path through the forest is familiar to all the rats, although Uphrasia and Konrad are the only ones to recognise the route they take alongside the human's floodlit vegetable garden. After a few hours more marching even General Scrod does not recognise anything familiar at all. After another hour they stop for a rest so that Abler and Scrod can consult the map and work out the best way forward. Scrod frowns as he studies the map. "We've never been this far west of the plant Professor, we had better keep our wits about us."

"You expect predators?"

"I do! There are far too many of us not to make a strong scent. I've had the feeling something has been following us for some time now."

Abler rubs his chin and places his skinny finger on the map pointing to where the forest ends and a wide open space of nothing begins, a dotted line leads across it to a crude drawing of a spaceship. "The wastelands will be the greatest challenge for the smaller ones."

"We'll have to figure something out for them." Scrod folds up the map, clears his throat and puffs up his chest. "Gather round all of you!" The band of around ninety rats all make a large circle around him and Abler. "I want you all to listen very carefully to what I am about to say. We are going across the wasteland tomorrow: a wilderness of great danger with no food or shelter for many miles. You must all keep up and stay together." They all grumble and chatter. Scrod raises one paw. "I know you are all tired and weary, but we must move onwards to the edge of the forest to make camp so that we can cross the wasteland in daylight. Let's move out rats!"

The smaller rats are lead out by Professor Abler and Nute who drag a cart full of equipment between them. The larger rats follow, headed by the seven remaining Zucker rats, then a mixed group of black, brown and fancy rats make up the rear guard. Uphrasia and Konrad follow up at the back. Konrad yawns and scratches his chest through his tunic. "All this marching is making me hungry. Do you think there will be a hot meal when we make camp?"

"Konrad, I doubt there will be any food when we get to camp."

"Oh, of course. No one to cook for us, all dead."

"Here." Uphrasia opens his tunic pocket and takes out a flapjack. "I kept one for the journey. Take it."

Konrad looks at the flapjack then frowns up at Uphrasia. "I couldn't. That's one of the ones…"

"Yes. The last flapjack my mother made. Look she'd want us to share it. Come on I'll split it with you."

The edges of Konrad's mouth turn down. "Well OK. Only because she'd want us to eat it and because I'm very, very hungry."

Uphrasia breaks it in two and gives one half to Konrad. Konrad waits for Uphrasia to take a bite, then eats his half.

They march through the forest, heading west. The path has gone now so they have to struggle through thick undergrowth and thorny brambles. They keep close. The smaller rats are linked together by a rope tied round their left paws. The others stick together looking all around for danger and predators. As night falls there are many strange sounds in the dark blackness beyond the feint light of the rat's tiny torches. Konrad shakes his torch and it flickers on and off. "Darn batteries are flat again."

Uphrasia moves behind him and shines his torch over Konrad's shoulder and they follow the group this way for a mile or so until Scrod raises his paw and shouts. "Halt!" All the rats stop and catch up with him. They find themselves in a clearing next to a fallen tree that has rotted on one side making a natural wall. "We will make camp here. It's too dark to proceed safely. Gather wood and forage for food. Remember your training and don't stray too far from the light of the fire. Rose and Nute fetch water." He gives Rose a large plastic bottle in a net sling. Rose and Nute carry it between them and head off into the trees. It is not long before they find a trickling brook. Rats have an enhanced sense of smell and can always find water or sniff out something to eat when they need it. Nute looks up at the tree canopy, her face betraying her feeling that she has the world on her shoulders.

Rose watches her intently. "What are your wires telling you?"

Nute looks down into the trickling water. "Nothing good. I think we should stay close to the General tomorrow. The wasteland is full of death!" Rose dips the bottle in the stream and it fills. Then they screw the lid on, place it in the sling and carry it back to camp in silence.

When they get back to camp all the other rats are sitting round the fire toasting worms and slugs over the flames. They plonk the water bottle down and Scrod gives them each a twig with a fat slug on the tip. "Well done." They take their place beside

Uphrasia and Konrad and hold their supper over the fire. Rose looks sideways at Uphrasia and he shuffles about and clears his throat.

"You found that water fast."

"Uh hum."

"That was. That was good foraging skills."

"Yep." They stare into the fire for a moment.

"I'm sorry about our date."

"It's OK. I mean we understand you were held up with foraging detention. Just as well as it turned out."

Konrad munches on a crispy worm. "We saw a dead crow when we were foraging just now. It was covered in maggots and really stinky!"

Rose frowns. "Right... Well it was good to catch up." She and Nute get up and move around to the other side of the fire.

Uphrasia nudges Konrad in the ribs. "Why did you mention that dead crow?"

"I don't know I was just making small talk."

"Well you scared them away."

"Well I'm sorry. I told you I can't talk to girls."

"Well then don't."

"Well I won't."

"Fine then."

"Right then." They both chew on their crispy worms and stare into the flames.

Scout forages in the dark forest. He spots a white grub under a log and picks it up and sniffs it. It wiggles loose and drops onto the ground and rolls down a slope. Scout follows it and then trips and tumbles down head over paws after it. He lands with a bump on a tree root and knocks himself out. The grub crawls slowly away and disappears under a leaf.

The morning sun peeks through the leaf canopy as the rats break camp and pack up their things. They line up for a swift inspection then they all march off in double time towards the edge of the forest. The trees give way to the open wasteland and Scrod narrows his eyes looking into the distance. Then when they are all lined up he gives the order. "Rats! On the double! March!" They all march out onto the plain, no one looks back.

About an hour later Scout comes round, he rubs his aching head. "Oh!" He stands up, staggers around a little then looks up at the waving trees. "I'm lost!" For about ten minutes he gathers his senses then climbs back up the bank to find his bearings. He recognises the log where he found that grub the night before. He crouches down and looks at the ground. Feeling with his paws he finds a footprint; it's his own. He follows his tracks and eventually arrives at the deserted camp. The fire is cold as he feels through the ashes with his foot. "Gone a few hours." Scout looks up at the sun shining through the trees, then he looks at the nearest tree and feels around the trunk for moss. Moss usually grows on the northern side of a tree where it is shaded from the sun. Scout takes a bearing from his path to the camp and using the sun and the moss he estimates west and heads out in that direction. He soon reaches the edge of the forest and looks out at the vast wasteland that stretches as far as the horizon. On the dusty ground are many little rat footprints heading west. He does not hesitate but marches confidently out into the vast deserted space. A while later a fox wanders into the abandoned camp and starts to sniff around. She is a vixen and she is hungry. She soon picks up Scout's scent and follows his trail to the edge of the forest. Normally she would not venture out into the wastelands but there has been nothing to hunt for several days. Pushed on by hunger she trots out over the dusty plain.

Out on the exposed plain the wind picks up clouds of dust and blows it into their eyes as they march. It is icy cold and their feet are numb and their paws are blue. At night there is no shelter for the rats to sleep under, so they all gather together in a huddle. The first night is quiet and although it snowed again, the huddle was warm. They heard the hoot of the owl but it did not discover them. The second night however is not so good. The owl came and took one of the smaller recruits in the darkness. No one heard it come or saw it go; just the blood-stained space where the rat had been the night before. The next night they do not stop to sleep but keep going all night. At around dawn they reach a small mound of tyres and find some shelter there. They huddle together inside the tyres and soon all fall into a deep sleep.

Scout wanders on alone, guarding his eyes with his paw from the icy wind and dust. He loses his sense of direction and strays off course. A stroke of luck as it happens because the fox barely misses him as it passes by. It picks up the scent of the other rats and begins to run.

The fox arrives at the tyre dump and starts to hunt around, sniffing and digging until it finds a young female fancy rat, one of Scout's group. The fox carries her off into the darkness. The other rats stare out from their hiding places with wide frightened eyes and no one sleeps a wink from that point on. Scrod gathers the group for a head count and has to make some tough choices. "We have taken some losses. The fox will no doubt return so we must divide into groups." He takes out the map and they gather round. "We are here and the space port is this way to the west. I will lead the strongest and fittest rats in a diversionary route while the weaker and smaller rats will make a dash for the space port in a straight line. 'Ten-shun!" They all stand to attention and line up for an inspection. Scrod walks along the line checking their uniforms and patting the smaller ones on the head. "I am proud to count myself among you brave young rats today. We all know what is at stake so let's not delay. Scout!" There is no reply. "Scout?!" All the other rats look around. Scrod frowns and folds his arms. "Ah. Well then, Professor, Rose and Nute will lead the first group. Take your team and all the smaller rats directly to the space port and get aboard as soon as you arrive. Hurry now!" They salute him and lead the group away up a short gradient and then pause at the top to look back once at their comrades, then they disappear over the horizon. The remaining rats get busy covering up their tracks and making new scent paths to confuse the fox. Then Scrod calls them into a small circle. "I did not want to share this with you while the smaller rats were with us. I have to tell you that our plan is far more dangerous than I first explained. We stronger rats will split up into two separate teams. I will lead one team northwards with all the equipment before making our way to the space port. Team two, you wait here until the fox comes into view, then run southwards leading her off and make your way northwest to the space port. I know this will be a perilous mission for the brave few who remain here. I wish there was another way but a fox is a determined predator and it will not stop until it kills us all! Some of you may not make it. It's a tough call but I have to select this team based on physical fitness and aptitude for this task."

Uphrasia and Konrad sit on the top of the tyre dump watching the horizon to the east, towards Grumthorpe and the inevitable return of the fox.

"Strange that General Scrod volunteered us for this important mission 'ay Uphrasia."

"Yes, he seems to have picked us out from the crowd."

Two Zucker rats and a young brown rat sit on the plain a short distance away also watching intently.

*Rats have poor eyesight and they are colour blind, so they struggle with spotting things of contrasting colour in a confusing background. Birds in the sky they can spot, as they can pick out dark objects against a light background. So it was no surprise that they did not spot the fox until it was very close.*

Konrad shuffles about on his bottom trying to get comfy on the hard rubber. "Is that a fox?"

Uphrasia sighs. "No that's a duck." He shakes his head. "Foxes can't fly Konrad."

"Oh. Is that a fox?"

"No, that's a large rock."

"How about that, that's a fox right?"

"No Konrad. Wait a moment that is a fox! Run!!"

Before the other rats are on their feet the fox snatches one of the Zucker rats and shakes him in its mouth killing him instantly. The others run up and over the tyre dump and follow Uphrasia and Konrad who are already racing south along the black earth on all fours in a cloud of dust. The fox digs a small hole in the ground and buries the Zucker rat, she'll be back for that later. Then she climbs up and over the tyre dump and looks southwards, sniffs the air and licks her lips. The plan has worked, she hops down and runs off at a steady pace southwards after them. She does not rush, she knows their small legs will not get them very far, so she conserves her energy. The rats run as fast as they can over the dusty ground. Uphrasia pauses to look back. The other two rats are about ten metres behind and the fox another thirty behind them. "She's gaining on us!"

Konrad puffs. "I don't know how long I can keep this up! I'm just not built for speed!"

"We have to keep going buddy! Come on!"


A gigantic mountain of garbage sits in the centre of the plain made up of tons of junk discarded by the humans of Grumthorpe. There is everything here, old cookers, motorbikes, garbage and tons of plastic, and on the very top a bright red stunt kite flaps in the wind tied with a pair of strings to an old, rusty metal rocking horse. Each day tons more garbage gets delivered by a steady stream of garbage trucks. They back up and tip up their loads then a man operating a tall crane lifts it up and places it on the very top of the mound. Then they all depart and head back to Grumthorpe as nights in the wastelands are not safe for anyone, not even humans.

Amid this dump of human waste a few creatures eke out a life. A few mice, cockroaches, beetles and ants scour the latest loads for morsels of food. At the bottom of the mound a small opening has been cleared away leading down a shallow slope to a dark hole. There is a scratching sound and out of this hole fly tin cans, old food cartons and soil. A huge feral badger backs out pulling a pile of old bedding made from torn up paper and plastic carrier bags. She has scars on her face and long, sharp canine teeth that poke down from her upper jaw. She carefully tidies up the entrance – badgers are very house proud – then sniffs around the dump looking for a tasty breakfast. Today there is not a lot around as it is Sunday and the garbage workers have the day off. So she digs around the border of the mound for worms and grubs. Scant pickings for such a proud and dangerous hunter. As her tummy rumbles with hunger she remembers chasing rabbits and stealing chickens from the local farms, before they all closed down. The last one was over six miles away and bit by bit the wastelands encroached and swallowed it up. After about an hour of searching and finding nothing she sits at the entrance of her set and warms up in the feint winter sunshine listening to the wind whistling through the gaps in the garbage above.

Back out on the plain the chase continues. Uphrasia notices the great mound rising up in the distance as they get closer to it.

"Konrad! Over there!"

"Can't! Have to stop!" They stop running and Konrad leans on Uphrasia's shoulder puffing and sweating. "You go on. I can't make it buddy!"

"Look, there is cover up ahead, just a bit further Konrad! You can make it. I know you can."

Konrad catches his breath. "OK. I'll try."

"Good rat!" They set off again in the direction of the mound.

Further back the Zucker rat knows the game is almost up. He looks across at the brown rat who is keeping pace with him. "Hey! What's your name?"

"Tray! What's yours?"

"Never mind that. Listen! I'm a Zucker rat right!"

"Right!"

"So I'm supposed to be an officer. I'll be advanced faster than you."

Tray narrows his eyes. "And your point is?"

My point is that you should fall back, let the better rat go first, if you get my meaning!"

"Oh yeah. I get your meaning. Loud and clear! OK. I'll drop back then. Good luck!" With that Tray slows down and lets the Zucker rat pull ahead.

"Herm? I thought he'd put up a little bit of a fight."

Tray looks back to see the fox just five or six metres behind and gaining fast. Then he leaps forward and lands on the Zucker rat's tail. The Zucker rat stops dead in his tracks and Tray hops over his back and bounces off his head. He races off looking back to see the fox snap its teeth around the Zucker rat's neck. "Well you wanted to be first!"

Uphrasia and Konrad finally reach the trash mound. They climb up the garbage and hop in through a narrow hole. They slither through the smelly compressed metal and plastic, then pop out at the entrance of the badger's sett and come face to face with the badger. She roars at them and shows her vicious teeth. They back up into the tunnel just as she snaps her teeth at them narrowly missing Uphrasia's face. They make their way up the trash pile, through old pipes, squeezing between squashed shopping trollies and discarded bicycles. The badger digs and rips at the trash trying to get at them. They go deeper and deeper then squeeze under an old fridge. The badger loses their scent and lets out a vicious growl. She tries again to dig but the trash is far too compressed at this depth, so finally she gives up and heads back to the entrance of her sett, sits down and scowls up at the sun. Uphrasia and Konrad emerge near the very top of the mound. They pause, catch their breath and look back across the plain. Tray arrives at the base of the mound and hops into the same hole just in time as the fox snaps her teeth, barely missing his tail as it vanishes inside. The fox looks up; Uphrasia and Konrad look down at her. She starts to climb the mound. Uphrasia scans the mound, looking for refuge. He spots a short length of metal pipe, grabs Konrad by the scruff of the neck and shoves him inside. Then he looks back for Tray who is scrabbling up an old slippery fridge. He jumps off the end and runs, closely followed by the fox. Uphrasia shouts, "Come on rat! Get a move on, she's right behind you!" The fox slips on the fridge and slides back. She makes her way around it and clambers over the garbage. Uphrasia looks down the slope, the badger pops its head up over her sett, looks up at him and snarls. Suddenly Uphrasia looks focussed, he backs into the pipe and beckons Tray, who makes it just in the nick of time.

"Phew! I thought I was a goner then!" He puffs and huffs at the end of the pipe. Snap! The jaws of the fox dart into the pipe and snatch Tray out and with a shrill squeak he's gone!

Uphrasia and Konrad move to the middle of the pipe. The fox's eye peers in at them and she growls! Then she vanishes and re-appears at the other end. She tries to get her head in to reach them but the pipe is too narrow. She barks and growls then tries to get at them with her front paws! "Rock the pipe Konrad!" Uphrasia yells. "Come on!" They both put their paws against the inside of the pipe and rock back and forth. Outside, the fox leaps about around the pipe, hopping over it and then back again and barking and yelping. The pipe rocks, then it tips slowly forward, pauses for a moment, then rolls forward and down the slope gathering speed. The fox gives chase, biting the pipe and clawing at it with her paws. The pipe rolls faster and faster down the steep mound, bouncing and tumbling! The rats spin round and round inside.

Konrad wails. "Ah! I feel dizzy."

"Hang on! Brace yourself!" They stretch and grip the inside of the pipe.

The pipe bounces off a wooden crate and spins through the air then lands just above the badger's sett and races down the last twenty feet. Just at the moment when the badger pops up her head to see what the commotion is. The pipe hits her squarely in the face knocking her onto her back. The pipe rolls on out across the flat plain. The fox skids down the last few feet, hops over the sett and lands directly on top of the badger. There is a loud roar followed by a yelp! Uphrasia and Konrad pop their heads out of each end of the pipe just in time to see the sandy-red back legs of the fox disappearing over the soil mound and sliding down inside the dark badger's sett.

The two stumble out of the pipe and try walking but they are so dizzy they keep falling over. They lean on each other until they get back their balance. "I think I'm going to throw up." Konrad moans then takes a step forward and falls over again. Uphrasia helps him up. "Ta!"

"Welcome. Let's get some rest and after a nap we can move on."

They make their way around the badger's sett, giving it a wide berth, then climb back up the trash mountain, huddle together exhausted under the rocking horse, close their eyes and fall asleep to the sound of the kite flapping in the breeze.

The wind is blowing hard by the time Scout reaches the tyre dump and the sun is already low in the sky. He reaches the base of the tyres where the feint tracks end and sniffs around. He notices a patch of sandy-coloured fur poking out of the dusty soil. He clears enough away to recognise the body of the Zucker rat buried by the fox. "Poor fellow." He climbs up the steep pile of tyres and sits on the top contemplating his next move. After some deep thought, he sighs. "If I stay here I will miss the launch window. If I march through the night, I may get eaten by a predator." He starts to climb down the other side of the mound and soon picks up the tracks, some heading south and others north. He shakes his head, then marches directly west towards the setting sun. Then he starts to run, kicking up clouds of black dust. For a good three hours Scout makes his way across the dusty plain; talking to himself and convincing himself that the space port will be just over the next rise. A steep sand dune stands before him and he struggles up it until he reaches the top, weary and out of breath. From here he can see the faint glow of the space port in the far west. In the valley below him is a small water hole with a few scruffy shrubs around it. "What luck?!" Scout sets off down the steep dune and starts to roll head over heels. He lands at the bottom and steadies himself. Here and there are tufts of tall grass. He sniffs the air but there is no hint of a scent. He makes his way through the grass towards the pool. Two of the tufts of grass move behind him. He stops in his tracks and looks back. The grass is still; not a sound. He hops forward and crouches down at the edge of the pool and takes a thirsty drink. The tufts of grass move slowly and silently up behind him.

Uphrasia shakes Konrad by the shoulders. "Wake up Konrad, we've slept too long, it's getting dark! We just have to get close enough to see the lights of the space port before the sun sets. Otherwise we're lost."

Konrad wipes his face with his arm and takes a big breath. "Alright, I'm awake. But I want to lodge formal notice that this is the last time I do any rushing about for a long, long time. OK? A long time!"

"Formal notice logged and understood."

Uphrasia looks to the west. "We're too far south so we need to head northwest or we'll miss the space port completely." He hears a flapping sound and looks up and sees the red kite darting about on the wind. "Maybe we can get a little help with that."

They rummage around in the garbage until Konrad finds the end of an old skateboard and tugs it free. He spins the wheels and the bearings are good. Uphrasia unties the kite, hauls it in and carries it down to the plain. He ties the strings to each of his wrists.

Konrad lashes Uphrasia's feet to the skateboard with some old rope, then he takes the kite out onto the plain and holds it up. "Ready?!"

Uphrasia lowers his head and braces himself. "Ready!" Konrad releases the kite and it falls to the ground. He picks it up again and holds it up as high as he can.

"Wait for a gust of wind!" Uphrasia yells impatiently.

Konrad waits, nothing happens, he sweats and huffs. Where is the wind? He steps to the left, then back to the right. Then the whiskers on his face blow back. He jumps up into the air and let's go of the kite. It rises rapidly, the edges vibrating in the strong breeze. Uphrasia feels a jolt and leans back, taking up the strain on the string. He lurches forward slowly, just a few inches. "I don't know if this will work Konrad!" Then he is tugged forward and the skateboard lifts up into the air, lands with a thud and races across the plain. Uphrasia steers, tilting the skateboard right and tugging on the right string of the kite to head northwest. The kite tilts and darts across the sky. Konrad starts to run to the left to intercept him. As Uphrasia bolts along, Konrad leaps and lands on the front of the skateboard. He holds on tight, lowering his head and closing his eyes as dust flies up into his face. The kite pulls them along faster and faster. They rise up a steep slope, jump over the top and fly through the air. "Ah...!" They land on the plain with a bump and shoot onwards, leaving a wake of dust and sand.

Scout lifts his head up and swallows the fresh water. "Ah!" Then two pairs of paws grab him by the shoulders, lift him up and turn him around to face two angry-looking ferrets! They have bright yellow grubby fur and large red eyes. One of them is a male and taller than the female. The male growls at him and sniffs his face, the female licks his fur then they lay him down, take his back legs and drag him through the grassy clumps towards a small dark hole in the side of the sand dune. Scout wriggles and squirms. "Please wait! I didn't mean to st-steal your water. Rats are rotten to eat I pro-promise you!" They drag him closer and closer to the dark hole. There is a loud flap above their heads and they look up to see the bright red kite shoot over them. They look at each other confused, then back up.

The skateboard slams right in between them sending them flying apart and they land stunned on the ground. Scout rolls onto his feet and sees Uphrasia and Konrad look back as they zoom across the water hole with a plume of surf, shouting together, "Sorry!"

Scout hops up, looks left and right and runs as fast as he can after them. He skirts around the pool and runs towards the distant glow in the west. After a good hour walking, Scout stops to catch his breath and looks up to see the bright shining floodlights of the space port no more than a mile away. If a predator came for him now he could not put up a fight. If he can just make it to the space port in time. He soldiers onwards, head down, still convincing himself to keep going. "Come on Scout. You can do this, just a few thousand rat paws to go." He stumbles and falls onto his face and puffs out blowing sand and dust up into the night air. "Just a few more…"

# Chapter 6
# INTERGALACTIC

The massive bulging hulk of the "PATRICK MOORE" intergalactic spacecraft is being fuelled in a huge dormant volcanic crater. Steam rises into a grey and moody dawn sky and low clouds obscure the tops of the four towering supports that keep the ship upright. The central body of the ship is a round cylinder around the inner core and is covered in white, heat-resistant tiles. A large rocket propulsion section sits under the central chamber. At the side of the ship is a sharp-pointed control cockpit that contains the ship's bridge. There is a huge metal disc on the very top. This ship has everything needed for a long voyage in space on its seven levels: plantations for growing crops, science labs, crew quarters for three hundred and sports facilities to keep them fit. There are bathrooms, toilets and a sewage treatment plant. All the levels are separated by shallow cavities that contain the air ventilation ducts. At the base of the ship is the nuclear power plant that drives all the ship's systems. Looking at it you might think that it would never get off the ground, weighing over a hundred tons when fully crewed.

Two tiny figures stand at the edge of the silo. Uphrasia and Konrad, hearts thumping in their chests admire the great ship. Uphrasia raises his bushy eyebrows. "A most impressive sight."

Konrad looks up at him and blinks. "I can't believe we made it this far. Us going into space after all we have faced. Will it fly?"

"I guess we are about to find out."

"Cor! Do you think it's true? Ratopia? Do you think we'll find it?"

"True or not, we deserve our place on this mission. We have evolved to a higher level. There is a greater understanding between us and all other species. We have elevated ourselves from our grubby, sewer-dwelling ancestors."

Konrad yawns a wide yawn. "Righto!"

They head down the slope and climb through a small hole in the base of the rusty perimeter fence. Then they walk along past fuel trucks and machinery when a technician in grey overalls spots them. He points and screams at the top of his voice, "Vermin!!"

"I believe some haste may be required Konrad!" Uphrasia snaps.

"Huh?"

"Run!"

They race across the silo as technicians try to stamp on them and wrenches and spanners clatter and bounce off the ground around them! They dart into a long copper pipe, hop out the other end and climb up a refuelling line. At the top Konrad hops about on the spot on the freezing pipe. "Oh, oh, chilly!" Uphrasia heaves him in through an open air duct. The duct is lined with heat-resistant silver foil. Wires droop down around Konrad's head. He shakes sweat off his snout, huffing and puffing.

Uphrasia pants. "It seems not everyone is in tune with our forward way of thinking."

"This mission seems to involve a hell of a lot of running around!" Konrad scratches behind his ear looking up at the mess of wires. "Is it safe?" He sniffs a bright red wire and licks it.

"Of course, technology has come a long way since the great disaster. But don't nibble any wires today Konrad. Uphrasia heads off along the duct.

Konrad licks the wire again then trots after him. "You hear so many horror stories," looking around nervously, "Ships exploding on take-off, asteroid collisions, ferocious aliens!?"

"Nonsense dear boy. They have high safety standards these days. Very high. This trip will be like a cruise ship holiday."

Konrad catches up with him. "With buffets of delicious invertebrates and molluscs!"

"Comfy deck loungers where we will be served cocktails and cockroach canapés!"

"Waited on paw and paw! Do you think I could get a pedicure? My toe nails are in a terrible state."

They come to a T-junction in the duct and bump into Thompus. They all stand looking at each other for a moment then Thompus heads off in one direction and they go off in the other. Uphrasia frowns. "Just don't know what to say to him."

Konrad wrinkles his snout. "Me neither. Awkward..."

"Mmm..."

The two climb out of a vent into a large junction of ducts where lots of other rats are milling around. General Scrod directs traffic. "Move along there. We have made makeshift quarters on this level. Family berths on the left, cadets on the right!"

Professor Abler walks along with Nute. "Now stay away from the nuclear reactor and keep your paws out of the sewer water. If you're not sure about anything, ask me."

"Oh Pappy, don't fuss over me. I'll be fine."

Uphrasia and Konrad peek out from behind a wall, one above the other. Uphrasia creeps out and whispers "Come on." As they tiptoe across the duct junction, Scrod spots them.

"You two!" They freeze in their tracks. "Yes, you! Over here now!"

Uphrasia puts on his most innocent look. "Who, us sir?" Konrad makes a loud gulp as they stand before Scrod.

"Ah ha! As I thought, the slackers! Private Teach and Private Konstantin!"

"Slackers? Us? No!" Uphrasia shakes his head.

Konrad shuffles from side to side. "Not us, sir."

"Humph! And how are we enjoying our morning?"

"Oh it's been very pleasant so far. Thank you for asking." Konrad is always very polite.

"Well, isn't that nice. And have you had a look over the lido, swimming pool and sauna section yet?"

They look at each other confused, Konrad sinks deeper into hot water. "No, we haven't yet. Which way is that please? I wouldn't mind a dip before evening rations."

Uphrasia closes his eyes and shakes his head.

Scrod shouts at the top of his voice with such power that Konrad's whiskers are blown back. "There isn't one, you weevil-infested excuse for a flea rug! Get to your quarters double-time. You should have been here hours ago, rotten, smelly, lazy scavengers!"

They scamper off. "He was a lot friendlier back at astro school!" Uphrasia pants.

"That must have been the soft sell. We're in for it now buddy!"

Scrod watches them go then smiles and nods. "I did not expect those two to make it. Well, well."

Thompus shuffles along a shiny metal duct. He notices a light up ahead coming through a vent. Through the vent is a brightly lit laboratory with a table filled with test tubes sitting in racks and a number of electronic gadgets sit on a long bench. He is startled by the sound of voices so backs away from the vent. He moves on along the duct until his path is blocked by a wire cage door. He sniffs at the door and pushes it with his paw and it swings back and forth with ease. He peers through the wire to see a large piece of chocolate sitting in the centre of the cage. Saliva drips from his open mouth. "Could be a trap." He pushes the door fully open and looks around inside it. It all seems safe. He edges into the cage and tries to reach for the chocolate. His paw is just a rat's foot too short of the tasty treat. "Herm..." He ponders the problem. Then he lifts up his right hind leg to hold open the door and leans forward until his front paw just grips the chocolate chunk. He tugs on it but it is stuck. He pulls harder and harder and it gives a little. Just under the chocolate chunk is a tiny thread of cotton attached to a small pin that sits in a hole. Thompus groans and pulls hard on the chunk and it gives way. The cotton pulls the pin out of its place and there is a loud click! Thompus freezes, looking left, right, up and down. Nothing happens. He shrugs and puts the chocolate in his mouth and chews. He exits the cage feeling very clever. Then the floor under his feet drops and he disappears. He slides down a long metal tube that curves round and round then opens into a square Perspex box. Thompus lands on a soft pile of sawdust and the opening over his head snaps shut. "Oh crumbs!" He gets up and feels around the walls of the box. "I'm in for it now! Wait! Remember your Space Corps elite training. Don't panic in any situation no matter how hopeless it may seem.

Remain calm at all times." Then he runs round in circles shouting. "Help, help, help, help, help!!!"

A technician counts down through a loudspeaker, his voice echoing round the space port. "Beginning countdown, beginning countdown in sixty seconds! All crew exit the launch area! All crew exit the launch area!" The staff load their equipment onto a long electric truck towing a row of low trailers. They all get on board and the vehicle exits the launch pad. The space port is silent apart from the creaking of metal and the sound of steam escaping the vents. "Commencing countdown! Twenty… nineteen… eighteen… seventeen…" In the packed launch control room men and women sit at consoles and operate the sensitive launch computers. On the large, oblong view screen, the Patrick Moore sits in the morning sun, steaming, silent, waiting. "Sixteen… fifteen… fourteen…" A deafening alarm horn blares out in the space port, warning everyone that the ship is about to blast off. "Thirteen… twelve… eleven…" Large sheets of ice begin to fall from the giant cooling pipes that pump freezing-cold liquid nitrogen around the engines to keep them cool. "Ten… nine… eight…" In the duct, the rats panic and dart off in various directions. In their new quarters, Uphrasia and Konrad strap into their posts on the padded floor. "Seven… six… five…" All the air vents on the outside of the ship start to close and seal with a hiss. All the interior doors swish shut and lock. Scout hops in through an air vent just before it snaps shut behind him! He collapses onto the floor, exhausted.

Konrad's teeth rattle as he tries to close the buckle on his strap. "Gorgonzola preserve us!" Outside, the huge ship begins to shake as the huge round disc at the very top starts to glow. A multi-coloured beam, the space anchor, rises up into the sky in a rainbow vortex.

"Four… three…" The ship shakes violently. "Two… one!" The space anchor extends towards the moon and encircles it with a glowing multi-coloured sphere. The support towers fall away with a great crash! The engines blast white hot flames and a great cloud of smoke fills the crater until the ship is concealed in it. The engines make a deafening roar, rising in pitch higher and higher! The great rattling hulk of the ship groans as it lifts slowly up and out of the crater. Metal grinds and cracks! "Lift off! We have lift off!" The ship rises out of the cloud of smoke and up out of the silo increasing in speed as it climbs into the clouds. The space anchor beam pulls the ship up out of the clouds and drags it up into space towards the moon. The ship strains as it pulls away from the earth's gravity. Then the engines cease and the ship jettisons the bottom half containing the lift-off engines. The beam pulls the ship faster and faster away from the Earth.

In their quarters, the two rats' faces begin to distort and flatten out. Then their bodies flatten too.

Konrad's body looks particularly odd as his tummy spreads out revealing the thin rat underneath. They both start to wail. "Ah...!"

The ship breaks free of the atmosphere and the space anchor vanishes. Rockets blast white fire and the ship slowly pulls away gathering speed until it arcs around the moon and darts off towards the Sun. The rats pop back into shape and Konrad holds his tummy. "Oh my lunch!"

Uphrasia looks shaken but pretends not to be. "Exhilarating!"

"I'm famished, let's get some breakfast." Konrad unstraps himself from his harness.

"I wouldn't do that if I were you buddy!"

Konrad floats up into the air. "Wee! I've always wanted to do this." He somersaults and bounces off the wall. "Woo, ha!"

Uphrasia watches tiredly, and remains strapped in. "Hmm."

Konrad cartwheels across the ceiling then bounces off the walls like a Ping-Pong ball. "He, he! Check this out!" He does a barrel roll then floats in the air doing an Egyptian walk.

"Konrad, seriously, you need to strap in."

"Awe come on. Live a little." He crouches down and does a funny walk along the ceiling. Uphrasia snorts with laughter.

The command bridge of the Patrick Moore is arranged in a semicircle with a view screen at the front. Above is the long cockpit window with a view out into space. There are eight humans on the bridge operating the various stations that include communication, navigation, weapons, long-range scanners and the ship's life support systems. Captain Villeroy sits in his command chair, firmly strapped in. He is tall with a chubby face, thinning fair hair and eyes a little too close together. He wears his smart beige uniform and his captain's cap. He speaks in a low, confident tone. "Ensign, activate centrifugal gravity!"

The ensign reaches over to his panel, his finger hovering over a round red button. "Activating centrifugal gravity, sir!" He presses the button and there is a loud rumbling sound. Outside jets of gas fire from the main circular section of the ship and it starts to spin slowly round and round the stationary central chamber.

Konrad slams into the floor head first with a mighty thud! "Ouch!"

Uphrasia shakes his head, then unstraps and looks out of the porthole. He smiles proudly and sighs. "Space! Our adventure begins!" Just then a large piece of metal floats past in flames. "That can't be good."

Konrad feels his round tummy and groans. "I've lost about four grams with all that rushing around. I'm going to need a lot of rations to make it all back up again."

Scout slowly comes round, he sits up and rubs his eyes, then climbs onto his feet and stumbles along the duct holding his head. He finds his comrades milling about in the main junction and staggers out a few steps, then flops down on the floor. A small group of concerned rats gather round him. Rose pushes her way through. "Stand back, stand back!" She lifts his head up. "Poor thing, he must be exhausted and half starved. Help me carry him to the med bay!" She lifts up his arms and a couple of lab rats take his feet and they carry him off.

The next morning Scout sits up in bed eating a bag full of freeze-dried, crispy fried worms. Rose and Nute stand next to his bed looking worried. "How do you feel now Scout?"

"Much, much better thank you Rose. These are v-very good."

"Would you like some more?"

He gives her the bag. "No thank you. I'm quite, quite full now. You have been very kind. I-I'm quite myself again."

Nute smiles. "If you are feeling well enough there is a very important mission on the cards. Nothing too strenuous."

Rose nods enthusiasm. "Yes and because you did so well finding your way across the wasteland alone."

"And defeating all those fearsome predators," Nute encourages.

Scout shakes his head. "All I really did was run away as fast as I could."

"Well, there is a scouting mission. We're all volunteering. The General wants a full survey done of the ship.

Rose puts her paw on his shoulder. "If you still feel poorly then you can rest up here for a few more days."

Scout kicks back the bed covers and swings his legs out onto the floor. "I'm quite w-well thank you. Sca- Scout's my name and sca-scouting's my game!"

Space travel is long and monotonous. Months pass slowly by without anything remarkable happening. Even what might seem a boring task, like cleaning up rat droppings from the ducts, becomes a welcome event. The rats amuse themselves as best they can, playing games like leaprat, hide-and-squeak, and fairy's-fair and fairy's-grim-which-paw-is-the-breadcrumbin? Nute spends many hours repairing and servicing the technical equipment with Professor Abler. Rose and Scout make several explorations of the ship and Scrod keeps everyone on their toes with marching drills and combat training. After several months of this they all get pretty restless. So whenever a real mission is rumoured to be on the cards all the rats get very excited; except for two particular rats that is. Uphrasia and Konrad are quite content collecting rat poo droppings in the ducts. They stroll along in their white overalls each with a brush in one paw and a long-handled dustpan in the other. Konrad hums happily to himself as he sweeps up a dry, round rat dropping into his dustpan. "The space rations are not bad, but the 'Easy Squeezy Cheezy Peas' are playing havoc with my digestion. Perhaps if they left out the cheesy part the squeezy peas would be OK. Or is it the peas?"

"You're not supposed to eat a whole tube at a time. They are super concentrated. Anyway stop talking about food, you're making me feel hungry." Uphrasia looks up at the ceiling. "What the?! How on earth?" He scrapes a rat poo off the ceiling and it drops down into his dustpan.

Scout stands in a duct with a large sheet of paper in his paw. He draws a crude map on it with a pencil. Then he places the pencil behind his ear and marches off along the duct. Soon he reaches a crossroads and looks left, right, then straight ahead. He ponders for a moment then opts to go left after drawing the new place on his map. At the end of this long duct Scout spots a grille on the floor with light shining through it. He hops up close to find a metal gate and just ahead of it an inviting-looking chunk of chocolate. Scout pushes the gate open with his paw and nods. "Obviously a trap." He makes a note of the trap on his map, then peers down through the vent.

The ship's science lab is a pristine white room with shelves upon shelves stacked with high-tech gizmos, gadgets, bottles of chemicals, large jars filled with invertebrates, amphibians and a rat in green formaldehyde liquid. Textbooks and files line the top-most shelf. It's a lot like Professor Abler's lab but much tidier. A small room is visible through a thick glass screen where a human in a radiation suit inserts his arms into two holes on the wall. On the other side of this wall the man's arms slide into thick rubber gloves. This is the ship's nuclear reactor station. The man pulls on a lever and in the sealed reactor room next door, a long plutonium rod is slowly inserted by a robotic arm into a hole on the opposite wall. The rod glows and a throbbing noise emanates from the hole.

Below the man's arms on the floor of the reactor, two rats, George and Agatha, sit on deckchairs wearing sunglasses, bathing in the heat of the reactor. "Awe, this is smashing George. Do you want me to rub some sun cream onto your ears?" Agatha holds out a tube of sun cream. The top is stained and has rat hairs all over it.

"No, I'm fine dear, just enjoying these rays. Better than the Costa del Sol, I can tell you!" George wriggles, adjusts his sunglasses and gets comfy, then smiles up at the reactor. "Better than the Costa del Sol."

Back in the science lab on a worktop in the corner is a transparent box, inside which Thompus slumps against the back wall with his eyes closed. He has a large round biscuit resting on his tummy. There is a grey plastic dome on his head and a memory chip sits in a slot in the side. Three thin wires attached to the dome lead up through a hole in the top of his Perspex prison. They wind their way along the lab table and into a large console covered in flashing lights and buttons. There is a small view screen in the centre next to a large lever.

Professor Fenkle, with crazy grey hair that stands on end, wears a white lab coat with several pens and pencils in the breast pocket. He has a long thin face and a bent nose. He looks through a big magnifying glass at Thompus. Fenkle's blue right eye is magnified to ten times its normal size. "The subject seems to be sedated. The formula has begun to work. Have you checked the box is secure Ilonja?"

Ilonja is pale and in her thirties and also wears a white lab coat. She has red hair tied into a neat bun on top of her head and large buck teeth. She peers over a clipboard through thick round spectacles. In an Eastern European accent, she says sharply, "I have checked and re-checked Professor; the case is secure! Nothing could escape from this box, not even a cunning, vile, sneaky, verminous little rat!"

"Excellent; then I think we are safe to proceed. Let's see how much information his tiny brain can contain? Begin the file download!" Fenkle rubs his hands together and grins. "Start with the files on the ship's schematics, then the complete works of Shakespeare. Oh and let's throw in a few hundred recipe books while we're at it."

Ilonja pulls on a large lever on the console. There is a loud buzz followed by an electric hum. "Beginning the download Professor!" The grey dome on Thompus' head starts to glow. His whole body begins to convulse and shake. Files and documents show up on the screen of the console. Then Professor Fenkle looks puzzled as some pictures of him doing a selfie appear.

"Ilonja, are those my private files?!"

Ilonja squints at the screen. "Oh! It seems I have accidently added your personal files. And what are these? They appear to be some images from a vintage lady's fashion journal on lingerie. I can't think why this has happened."

Fenkle clears his throat. "U-hum! Well never mind that. Let us see how much of his brain has been filled up so far. He quickly flicks a switch and the picture on the screen changes to an image of Thompus' brain. The bottom half is coloured red and the top half is grey. "Well it seems to be working. We will let him assimilate the information he has so far and then fill up the memory card with even more files this afternoon. This is so diabolical it makes me proud to call myself a scientist!"

Ilonja wipes a tear from her eye and blubs. "So proud! So very proud!"

Thompus groans with his eyes tightly closed he mumbles. "But, soft! what light through yonder window breaks?"

Scout watches through the ventilation grill above. "M-m-must report this atrocity to g-g-General Scrod at once!" He stuffs his mao in his rucksack then skitters along the metal ventilation duct on all fours.

In a distant part of space, a small alien spaceship floats serenely through a cluster of planets. It is black and pointy with three large, curved and jagged fins on the back end. There is a small round hatch on the top behind a clear dome that is lit from within. At the back three conical rocket engines are fixed to a round platform. They glow red as the ship cruises along. On the side is a crudely painted name, "THE VANDAL!" The bridge is cramped and made out of metal with red iron beams perforated with holes which curve up and join at the centre of the ceiling. Nets hang between the beams filled with red and yellow fruit, green vegetables and large round nuts. Four control consoles are arranged in a square, with one large screen at the front showing a view of space. Stars whizz past as a small planet gets closer and closer. Five round aliens operate the controls. They have multi-coloured stripes on their gelatinous bodies, no neck and a single antenna on the middle of their heads above three large round eyes. They pull levers and press various glowing buttons on their individual work stations. Their voices are loud and raspy as they chatter to each other.

First Mate Carak has white stripes on his bright orange body. He grunts and grinds his teeth as he operates the controls and levers of the weapons and long-range scanning station. Gark and Tark are identical twins and have black stripes on their white bodies. They operate the ship's navigation station together. They constantly argue with each other despite being inseparable. Spigot, who is slim and has yellow stripes all over his green body, manages the ship's life support systems and catering station. He is always on a diet and is the only one who can be trusted not to eat everything.

Carak spins round. "Captain, I have detected a planet with a small number of emerging life forms."

Captain Bibulous, the largest of the aliens, has blue stripes on his light-grey body and a broken antenna with a bandage covering the break. His face has scars on it and he has a very large mouth. He swings his command chair round and grins, showing a row of yellow-stained pointy teeth. He glares with his three fierce eyes. "Show me! On the main view screen! Now!" He turns back to look up at the big monitor as a planet much like Earth appears. He taps away at his console and the planet gets bigger on the screen. Again he taps and the screen zooms into the planet's surface. Luscious green meadows, lakes and forests appear. Bibulous taps again and zooms in to view some creatures drinking water from a small stream. They are mammals with soft grey fur, short snouts, small round eyes and long, thin, hairless tails. One of them nuzzles its snout into the side of the other. Bibulous drums his fingers on the console and purses his lips. "Hmm…" All the other aliens look at him expectantly then at each other. Will he, won't he? Bibulous stands up and paces back and forth across the bridge. "A planet full of new and innocent life forms just on the brink of reaching their full potential. Such a beautiful place. One could imagine living there, raising a family. Summer holidays at the seaside." He rests his hand on Carak's shoulder and smiles serenely at him. "Telling bedtime stories at the fireside with the children. Ah…" He jumps back onto his chair and spins back round to face the main view screen, eyes wide and teeth clenched. "Activate the Obliterator!"

They all cheer.

Carak presses a button on his console. Outside on the top of the ship the clear round hatch slides open and a giant laser mounted on a transparent turret full of coloured wires rises up. The laser glows with a bright white pulsing light that moves along the long, pointy barrel to the tip where it vaporises in space with a loud zap, zap, zap, zap!

Bibulous' eyes widen and he grins an evil grin. "Charge the Obliterator!"

Carak giggles. "I love it when he says that." He presses another button and pulls down a long lever.

"Charging the Obliterator!" The laser glows brighter and brighter. With a loud, pulsing throb, the zaps repeat faster and faster. Carak stares at a meter as a needle moves slowly from left to right and enters a zone marked in red. "Obliterator charged at full power, Captain!"

Bibulous stares wide eyed at the big monitor, his tongue hanging out. "Are we ready?!"

They all shout together. "Yes, Captain!"

Bibulous grits his teeth. "Obliterate!!!"

Carak slams his fist on a large, round, red button! "Obliterate!" he screeches!

The weapon fires a bright bolt of white light that widens and fans out towards the planet. The planet explodes into a mass of tiny bright pinpoints and then vanishes inwards with a loud pop! A small pinpoint of light glows, then brightens, then BOOM! A mighty explosion is followed by a massive energy wave that spreads out across space.

The Vandal is shaken, spins round like a twig in a whirlpool, then settles. All the aliens roll around on the floor laughing hysterically. Carak climbs up onto his chair and spins round and round. "That was so cool!"

Gark and Tark lean on each other laughing hysterically and Spigot lies on his back drumming the floor with his feet. "Let's blow up another, another!"

Bibulous stops laughing abruptly. "No! I have had enough of obliterating meagre planets. I want something more!" He stands up, waving his chubby hands in the air.

Carak's face turns serious. "Yes, evil prankster?! What do you want to obliterate?"

Bibulous paces back and forth. "More!"

All of them suddenly show keen interest. "Yes – yes!"

He flops in his chair. "I do not know." They go back to their seats, disappointed. Bibulous holds his head in his hands. "How can I maintain my reputation as the great Bilothian, Bibulous, destroyer of the innocent, harbinger of death, despondency, desolation and despair! The voluminous perpetrator, the globulous galactic?" He clicks his fingers looking for a word. "Thingemygig! Basically the evillest being in the whole universe!"

Carak interjects. "Known universe."

"If I can't find something meaningful to destroy, something wicked? Something…" Bibulous' eyes go wide. "Stupendously diabolical!!"

The Bilothians are a troubling species. They love to make war on each other and really love seeing things blow up. It all began as a practical joke when one Bilothian dropped a giant blancmange on another's head. It all escalated until several years ago two warring tribes blew up their home planet. Now the remnants of their race are scattered about the universe, stealing, vandalising and destroying whatever they can find. Especially if it makes a very large explosion; the larger the better!

The others huddle together and chatter, then push Carak forward "How about a nebular?" he suggests. "They are full of explosive gasses I think?" He puts his forefinger into the hole in his antenna; a common thing Bilothians do when thinking hard.

Bibulous paces back and forth. "Been there, done that!"

Carak tries again. "What about a red dwarf, a sun?!"

They all grunt their enthusiasm for this idea, and Gark screeches, "Or a black hole!"

Tark disagrees and they start to argue. "Black holes are boring!"

"They are not! They are brilliant!"

"How can they be brilliant if they are black? Numbskull!"

Carak starts throwing in quick-fire suggestions. "A pulsar! "A quasar! A Spiral galaxy! An asteroid cluster!" He punches the air. "I've got it: a micro universe!" He holds his finger and thumb together and stares at the tiny gap between them. "They are very, very small but make a ginormous ka-boom!" He slams his fist onto his other hand "Boom!"

Bibulous cuts him off. "No, no, no! I want to blow up something special." He sighs looking dejected. "Planets and celestial bodies have lost their charm for me. Where is the thrill of the chase? They just sit there. They don't flee or defend themselves. Where is the fun in that? No! I need something..." He moves his hands around searching for the word in his mind then slams his fist on the console. "I don't know! But we are searching the universe until we find it! Back to your stations. Activate long-range scanners Carak!" He rubs his hands together as they all rush to their posts. "I have a feeling in my swollen, rancid gut that the perfect thing is heading my way."

The Patrick Moore drifts past a cluster of asteroids then reverse thrusters fire and it slows down to a stop. At the front section, just below the cockpit on the non-revolving part of the ship, a large cargo bay door opens. A giant robotic arm rises up and extends out towards the asteroids. Its massive claw-like hand opens. Then three fingers and one opposing thumb close around a small asteroid with a loud crunch. It retracts back into the cargo bay and places the asteroid on the deck. The doors creak closed and seal with a loud hiss.

In a small, cramped room, Uphrasia and Konrad sit among a group of uniformed rats on a row of long benches while Scrod briefs them. He uses a long pointy toothpick to indicate a crude diagram of Thompus in his Perspex prison.

"This is our lost comrade and the target for this extraction mission. He doesn't seem to be in too much distress but be on guard. The subject may be mentally scarred by the constant and cruel experiments carried out by these evil and ruthless human scum!" Scrod places the toothpick under his armpit and gives them all a hard searching stare. "I will need brave volunteers for this heroic and highly dangerous mission." He diverts his attention to Uphrasia and Konrad, staring hard with his round black eyes.

Uphrasia whispers through the side of his mouth. "Don't move a muscle or he'll pick us."

Konrad pipes up. "Pick us?!"

"Well done Konrad and Uphrasia! You brave young chaps are real gung-ho heroes."

Uphrasia puts his head in his paws. "Not again?"

Scrod points at Rose with his stick. "Rose can give technical support."

Rose smiles and bats her eyelashes at Uphrasia.

Uphrasia groans under his breath. "Add to my humiliation."

"Scout will guide you to the extraction point!" Scrod puts the toothpick back under his armpit and grins. "Good luck, and if you don't come back alive we'll honour your memories with a huge feast."

All the other rats cheer and applaud.


Scout leads the way as Uphrasia, Konrad and Rose shuffle along a narrow duct wearing simple leather tool belts, carrying ropes, block and tackle. Konrad carries a large red drill with a spinning disc.

"It's just not fair. If we don't come back alive we're going to miss out on a huge feast in our honour. Why us, what did we do?"

Uphrasia grits his teeth. "I think we made a bad impression."

Rose halts. "That's it! If we make a fine job of this mission, we are sure to get into Scrod's good books."

Konrad plays with the drill, spinning it twice. VRUM, VRUM! "Yes, all we need to do is rescue Thompus. How hard can that be?"

As Uphrasia walks along the drill buzzes again. VRUM!! He stops abruptly. "Ouch!"

Konrad hides the drill behind his back. "Oh cripes!" A tuft of fluffy brown hair is stuck to the drill disc. Uphrasia cranes around and looks at his backside where a perfectly round patch of bare pink skin is exposed. He scowls at Konrad who forces an innocent smile. "Sorry. It just, sort of, went off in my paw."

Rose sniggers. "Oh Gorgonzola, that's so embarrassing."

"Give that to me!" Uphrasia snatches the drill. "I will handle the power tools from now on!" He stomps off along the duct.

Konrad looks back at Rose and they giggle.

They arrive at the vent and Konrad notices the lump of chocolate a few inches away. "Couldn't we just go over and have a nibble?"

Scout pulls the metal gate closed. "It's a trap! No touching the chocolate Konrad!" They start work drilling out the screws that hold the vent grille in place. Konrad keeps glancing back at the chocolate chunk and his tummy rumbles.

The lab is deserted. Thompus sleeps soundly in his plastic prison. The ventilation grill rattles and creaks, then swings aside revealing the four rats' faces looking down. Scout lowers two ropes and Uphrasia and Konrad abseil down onto the lab table while Rose attaches the block and tackle to the top of the ventilation grille. Uphrasia hops along the lab table and peers in at Thompus. "The fool. How did he get into this mess?" He sets to work drilling a large round hole in the side of the box. Konrad looks at Thompus through the Perspex. "Is he dead?"

"Let's hope so, then we can get the hell out of here."

"Don't you find this ironic?"

"Ironic how?"

"Well, us two ne'er do wells rescuing an elite Zucker rat."

"I don't think this one counts as elite."

Konrad sniffs the air. He looks over to his left and spies a sandwich on a plate a few rat paws away. He scampers over and sniffs the neatly prepared meal. His mouth waters and his tongue hangs out. He can't resist. Just as he takes a bite, Ilonja picks up the sandwich and also takes a big bite. She freezes, seeing

Konrad's face close up, his teeth gripping the other side of the sandwich. Ilonja' stares at him for a moment, a long, long, frozen moment. Konrad raises one eyebrow. "Hmm."

Ilonja screams at the top of her voice. "VERMIN!!!" She flings the sandwich with Konrad still clamped onto it across the room. Konrad spins through the air and lands on top of the plastic box and the sandwich hits the back wall and sticks fast.

Uphrasia is tugging Thompus out through the small hole. "Konrad help me!"

Ilonja jumps up on a chair and pulls up her lab coat around her knees. "Ah! Vermin, vermin, vermin!!!" She looks up at Rose and Scout who are heaving Thompus' limp body up with the block and tackle. "Ah!" She watches as Konrad and Uphrasia quickly climb their ropes and clamber back up into the duct. Dr Ilonja's knees shake and knock together. Then she faints and falls off the chair and says weakly "Vermin..." She hits the floor with a thud!

On the bridge all is calm. Captain Villeroy sits dozing in his command chair. An intercom on the arm of his chair beeps, startling him. His chubby finger presses a button and he speaks wearily, "Hello. Is that the kitchen? Is my hot chocolate ready?"

The thin panicky voice of Ilonja comes out of the tiny speaker. "Sir, this is Ilonja! Science officer! We have a vermin problem. An infestation!"

"Vermin?"

"That's not all, sir; they have taken our experimental subject."

"Is that a bad thing?"

"Affirmative sir. It's a very bad thing!"

"Oh bother. Tell Professor Fenkle to exterminate them! I'm very, very busy here." He switches off the intercom, folds his arms and closes his eyes. "Relax. Positive thoughts, positive thoughts."

Professor Fenkle enters the lab carrying a large box. He opens it taking out three smaller boxes, each with a logo of a rat with a lightning bolt going through it. "I suspect that we are dealing with a group of very intelligent rodents."

Ilonja's eyes are wide and her hands shake. "Do you think they're dangerous, Professor?"

"Most definitely! They represent a major threat to the success of our mission!" He cuts open a box with a scalpel.

Uphrasia, Konrad and Rose pant as they drag the unconscious Thompus along the duct. Rose huffs. "Phew, he's a heavy load! Is it possible he's gotten larger since we boarded this spacecraft?"

Uphrasia heaves. "Probably force fed by those sick fiends! I can smell success. I feel a medal coming my, I mean, our way."

Rose frowns. "You don't think we caused a bit of a stir back there? I mean, you know, that sandwich incident?"

"No… I doubt if they even noticed little old us." Scout remarks.

Konrad licks his lips. "That lady on the other end of my sandwich seemed pretty upset. She used the 'V' word."

Uphrasia shakes his head. "I doubt if they will worry about a few rodents rescuing this worthless heavyweight rat. I bet they are laughing about it all right now."

Professor Fenkle looks very serious as he opens one of the smaller boxes. "There you are my dear." In the darkness of the box, two red glowing eyes peer back. He reaches in, lifts out a robotic cat and looks it over. Its body is bright shining metal alloy with overlapping layers on its back like an armadillo. The head is like a cat's but has a strong brow with a hatch on it and a pair of red glowing eyes below. The legs are moved by pneumatic pistons and the tail is made of a long, flexible chain link. "Now, where is the ON switch? Ah, here." He flicks a switch under its neck and places it on the table. It starts to rattle and shake. Its sharp, serrated metal jaw snaps three times and it talks with a robotic voice. "Exterminate all vermin! Exterminate all vermin!"

Ilonja grins. "Will it kill all the rats Professor? Every single one?!"

"Not exactly Ilonja, I have programmed the Cybormoggies to use an immobilising laser. It will stun them, capture and bring them back here so we can experiment on them at our leisure.

Ilonja claps her hands. "An excellent plan, Professor. So wonderfully wicked! Although, after our terrible mistake with that subject earlier, should we continue with our horrible and vile experiments?"

"Well, we are scientists Ilonja. What else do we do if we don't make horrible, hideous life-threatening errors?" Ilonja nods her approval. Fenkle continues, "I can safely say that within twenty-four hours all the vermin on this ship will be dead or in a serious amount of pain! Ha, ha, ha, ha!"

Ilonja joins in, "Ha, ha, woo-ha, ha, ha!"

They both laugh demonically but Professor Fenkle gets carried away. "He, he, woo-ha, ha, ha, he, he, he, woo-ha, ha!"

Ilonja slaps him hard across the face and he stops laughing and pants. "Thank you, Dr Ilonja!"

"My pleasure, Professor Fenkle!"

"I appreciate your dedication."

"But it really was my pleasure." She looks at him with narrowed eyes.

Fenkle switches on another Cybormoggy. He places it on the floor. "I am a little worried, about all the sensitive information we downloaded into that rat's tiny brain."

Ilonja shrugs her shoulders. "So he knows how to find his way around and can steal a few rations. What harm can he do?"

"With the help of that chip in his head he can locate every morsel of food on this ship; plus, ship's schematics, security codes, weapons' operation and other rather sensitive information!" He frowns.

"Ah! That is serious."

Fenkle opens the third box. "Do not worry my dear Ilonja. I have unleashed the Cybormoggies. They will soon gather up all the rats. Then we will quickly dispose of them. Or worse!"

He gives Ilonja a sly, sideways look. She snorts and sniggers.

Ilonja rubs her hands together. "Professor, what will we do now that we have nothing to experiment on?"

The professor rubs his chin, then looks at her hands. "Hmm. How about your left hand?"

Ilonja claps her hands grinning. "Oh, an excellent idea! I'll fetch the sulphuric acid!"

Fenkle gets carried away again. "Ha, ha, ha, woo-ha, ha, he, woo-ha, ha!

She slaps him across the face again.

"Thank you, Dr Ilonja."

"My pleasure, Professor Fenkle!"

"Yes, I know, you are so very helpful."

"No, but it really was my pleasure." She narrows her eyes again and he frowns and looks left and right nervously.

# Chapter 7
# ATTACK OF THE CYBORMOGGIES

Uphrasia, Konrad and Rose are heaving Thompus along the duct followed by Scout carrying all the equipment.

They hear a drowsy voice. "Is it lunchtime yet?"

Rose drops her heavy load on the ground. "What?! You're awake?! We've been dragging your sorry carcass for hundreds of paws!"

Thompus rubs his behind. "Hey, I bruise easy!"

Uphrasia lets go too. "What happened to you?"

"When I last saw you guys I got caught in a rotten rat trap and those weird scientists did stuff to my brain." He points at the dome on his head and the chip protruding out of it. "Food was great though! That's what is so unfair about being experimented on by mad scientists. Great food, hideous torture. Great food, more hideous torture. Even more great food."

"Yeah we get the picture," Uphrasia interrupts.

Konrad tugs a breadcrumb out of his tummy fur and eats it. "He's not wrong. I wish I had finished my sandwich. It's way past lunchtime and I'm hungry. I don't mind telling you, I could eat a fridge, a whole ham or a bunch of bananas or a grain barge, even a shed-load of rotten old potatoes no one wants! Even if they did want them, I would eat the potatoes and the shed."

Uphrasia taps him on the shoulder. "Konrad?"

Konrad smiles up at him. "Was I doing that thing again?"

"Yes!"

"Sorry. I get carried away."

"I know."

Thompus' eyes glaze over and he starts talking in a strange dopey tone. "I know where the store of ship's biscuits is located."

Konrad's eyes bulge. "Ship's biscuits!"

Uphrasia helps Thompus to his feet. "How do you know that?"

Thompus in the same dreamy monotone explains. "For some reason, I know a lot of information that I am not supposed to know. Star fields, ship's schematics, crew health reports, a recipe for blueberry muffins and a picture of Professor Fenkle in lady's lingerie. It fills me with a deep and unbearable gloom."

Rose folds her arms and eyes him up and down suspiciously. "I don't know. It all sounds a bit fishy to me."

Thompus drones on. "There may be jam or marmalade. Yes, definitely jam."

Konrad clasps his paws together. "Ship's biscuits and jam! Oh it's too much for any rat to resist! We have to go!"

Rose tries to usher them forward. "The mission guys. Stick to the mission."

Konrad hops up and down. "We could grab a quick lunch, take Thompus back to Scrod by evening rations and get our medals. Let's go! Ship's biscuits, ship's biscuits, ship's biscuits, ship's biscuits, ship's biscuits, ship's biscuits!"

Uphrasia shakes him by the shoulders. "Konrad!"

"Sorry."

"Focus up."

"I am fully focused on the next stage of our mission – if it involves ship's biscuits!"

Rose puts her paws on her hips. "Guys, we should go straight back to General Scrod as per our orders! Report the location of the supplies so everyone can have a share."

Thompus gets up and shuffles his feet along the duct. "It's this way. Come along if you're hungry."

Uphrasia watches him go and frowns. "He's acting a little odd, don't you think?"

"I like him; he has his priorities right. Rat Way, remember?" Konrad marches off after him.

Rose gasps. "Yes, the great Rat Way – 'Eat what you want, take what you want, sleep where you want'. Don't you think it's a bit outdated?"

Uphrasia looks offended. "It's our way of life! Come on, let's eat!"

They follow Thompus leaving Rose and Scout standing. "Guys, this is wrong! We should stick to our mission! Follow our orders!" Rose lets out a big huff, then follows. "Come on Scout we better stick together."

The ship's store is a small square room stacked to the ceiling with plain brown cardboard boxes – all of which have been torn open. A few empty marmalade and jam jars lay on their sides. Uphrasia, Konrad and Thompus lie on the floor surrounded by crumbs. Konrad groans and rubs his bulging tummy. "Oh, I couldn't eat another thing."

Rose stands in the doorway with her arms folded "Just as well. You've eaten the whole lot! What about all the other rats on this ship?"

Uphrasia rolls onto his back. "First come, first served. We followed the Rat Way to the letter."

Scout sits in the corridor sketching out another map. "You're wasting your time Rose. There's no reasoning with them."

"You are all so selfish!"

Uphrasia props himself up on one arm. "You suggest we go against our own nature, against the wisdom passed down by all the great minds of our kind?"

"Great minds! What great minds?"

"The poets and playwrights: Ratsworth, Rodentspear? All the great thinkers: Socraties, Ratstein."

Konrad raises his paw, "Ratsputin?"

"Not a good example, Konrad."

"Sorry."

126

"Those are just human thinkers you have given rat names to. You are making it all up!" Rose boils over. "Ooh, I've had it with you lot!" She storms out of the room and along the corridor. "You're so exasperating!"

"What's eating her?" Thompus sighs.

"Certainly not ship's biscuits." Grins Konrad. "Such an unappreciated delight. It's the complete lack of flavour that makes them so delicious."

Uphrasia groans. "I think I'm going to throw up." They all laugh.

Konrad farts. "Uh oh, ship's air biscuit!"

Scout finishes his map, stands up and looks at them for a moment from the doorway. "You couldn't have saved me a morsel?"

Thompus shrugs. "Sorry pal you should have kept up with us."

Scout folds his map and heads off after Rose.


Two of the Cybormoggies walk along the corridor, their gears and motors whirring, red eyes glowing, scanning all around. They arrive at a door with a sign on it, "SHIP'S STORE, RESTRICTED". The door is slightly ajar and light shines from within. The Cybormoggies leap into the room, the hatches on their heads pop open and tiny lasers rise up and dart around looking for a target. The room is empty except for empty jars, cardboard boxes and crumbs.

The three rats stumble along a metal air duct arm in arm supporting each other. "Rose sure is grumpy today," remarks Uphrasia.

Thompus winks at Konrad. "I think that fancy rat fancies Uphrasia."

"Get away! She does not. She hates me, clearly."

"The lady doth protest too much!" Thompus shouts. "She is a woman, therefore may be woo'd; She is a woman, therefore may be won!"

Konrad licks his chest fur. "I hope we don't get any more missions. I'm worn out."

Uphrasia raises up his snout proudly. "We've done our duty. That's it now. We ride the gravy train and no more volunteering, OK?"

"OK!" Konrad burps. "Unless a mission ends up like this one resulting in another great feast."

"Not even if there is a possibility of a food reward. We have had our fill of danger and adventure. It's back to collecting rat droppings from now on. OK?"

Konrad shrugs. "If you say so."

There is a very large void under the ship's cargo bay with long, white metal girders supporting the heavy cargo floor above. The area is full of rats socialising and playing games together. An old grey rat plays honky-tonk on a toy piano while Nute dances with an imaginary partner. Uphrasia and his friends hop out of an open vent. Konrad spots some rats playing. "Leap rat! I love that game; except it makes me hungry."

"Sleep makes you hungry," Uphrasia chuckles.

Drawn by the noise, a Cybormoggy heads along a duct towards the junction. Its right ear swivels left and right, filtering the noise to identify the individual sounds. It walks up to the end of the duct and peers through the grille, scanning the scene. On its internal view screen, it identifies the heat images of the rats. Each individual rat freezes on the screen and the flashing words identifying each one appear: "Rattus rattus", "Rattus norvegicus", "fancy rat" and "Zucker rat". "Exterminate all vermin!" the robotic voice commands. The grille bursts open and the Cybormoggy leaps out, lands on the piano and fires laser bolts at random, zapping rats here and there. It zaps the pianist and he flops down under the piano. All the rats panic and run in different directions bumping into each other, scattering and darting into vents or hiding behind any cover they can find. The Cybormoggy jumps down and hops around firing at anything that moves. "Exterminate all vermin! Exterminate all vermin!"

Nute dives under the piano followed by Uphrasia, Konrad and Thompus. Nute grabs Uphrasia's arm. "Try to distract it! There has to be a power switch to turn it off somewhere!"

"Distract, how?!"

"I don't know but you have to do something!"

A laser bolt whizzes past the piano. Nute covers her wires with her paws. Uphrasia frowns and then an idea dawns and he wriggles backwards. "Konrad, can you still remember your dance moves?"

"I guess so. Why?"

"I have a crazy idea."

The Cybormoggy scans the room with its red glowing eyes. Suddenly Konrad hops up onto the piano and starts tap dancing while Nute plays the piano, keeping her head low. The Cybormoggy spots Konrad and on its internal viewing screen tries to target him with a crosshair. Konrad keeps hopping about and tapping out a rhythm with his toes. "So much for no more danger then!"

Uphrasia creeps along behind the unconscious bodies and up behind the Cybormoggy. He steadies himself.

Konrad starts to sing.

*"It's tough at the bottom of the food chain, when every single day is do or die, and whenever you look up, all you see is someone's butt, crapping down on you from on high!"*

Uphrasia leaps up on to the back of the Cybormoggy and holds on tight to the layers of armour. The Cybormoggy stops firing, cranes its head around a hundred and eighty degrees and glares at Uphrasia with its creepy red-glowing eyes. Uphrasia leaps forward and throws his arms around the Cybormoggy's neck. Nute and Thompus join in with Konrad, singing at the top of their lungs.

*"Yes, it's tough at the bottom of the food chain, when no one seems to care or wonder why. You're bound to stink a bit, when you're swimming round in Sh-oo-oo-wage. The scorn of every single passer-by."*

Nute shrieks. "It's working! Come on Uphrasia!"

The Cybormoggy flails its head around trying to shake Uphrasia off. It starts to buck like a bronco but he holds on tight. Then he slips and hangs under its neck. The laser fires, zap, zap, zap, missing Konrad's head by a hair. Uphrasia spots the switch on the underside of the Cybormoggy's chin. He reaches up but misses. Swinging left and right his back feet skitter on its chest. He reaches again and his fingertips brush the switch. A laser bolt hits the piano and Konrad leaps off. Konrad picks up a tennis ball and tosses it at the Cybormoggy and it bounces off its head. The head darts an angry look at him and the laser fires again and a bolt of white light just skims the tuft of hair on Konrad's head, leaving a smoking trench. One more desperate reach and Uphrasia grips the switch with both paws and hangs there. The Cybormoggy jerks left then right and Uphrasia swings, hanging on desperately. He swings his hind legs up and around the Cybormoggy's neck and heaves as hard as he can.

There is a click and the switch flips down. Uphrasia's paws slip and he falls and lands on his back. The Cybormoggy looks down at him, narrows its eyes and bows its head. The laser points directly at Uphrasia's face and he closes his eyes expecting the worst. The Cybormoggy snaps its jaws three times right at the tip of Uphrasia's snout, then it slowly tips forward and collapses on top of him.

The others rush over and Nute hops from one foot to the other. "He did it, he did it!"

A strained, muffled voice pleads from under the heavy machine. "Get this thing off of me!" They lift up the Cybormoggy and Thompus drags Uphrasia out by his arms. "Wow, that was dangerous even for a private in the Space Corps!" He pants and gets to his feet.

Nute takes a screwdriver out of her tool belt and unscrews a small hatch on the Cybormoggy's chest. She pulls it open and reaches inside. "Some kind of cybernetic cat." She pulls out a circuit board and inspects it. "Hmm. Elegant circuit work." She tugs and pulls out the hard drive and waves it about in the air. "Can I keep this?"

Konrad kicks the Cybormoggy. "What a scary cat! Do you think there are any more like that?"

"Let's hope not." Uphrasia brushes his fur down. "This adventure is starting to get a little too hectic for my liking."

After a long and boring briefing with General Scrod, both Uphrasia and Konrad get a well-earned rest in their quarters. Despite Uphrasia's warning, Konrad gobbles down three tubes of Easy Squeezy Cheesy Peas, seven slices of toast with jam and three dried, smoked slugs. Konrad explains that due to the increase in missions he needs more energy stores. They lay down on their sleeping posts and close their eyes.

Konrad looks across at Uphrasia. "There can't be any more missions now, can there?"

"Well if there are I doubt if our names will come up again."

"Phew I'm glad to hear it."

"Good night Konrad."

"Good night Uphrasia."

They close their eyes and fall asleep almost right away.

# Chapter 8

# MAROONED

The ship drifts through space towards a spiral solar system, then slows down and orbits round planet PLEKREL 375, which has orange and yellow horizontal stripes around its surface and two orbiting rings: one orange inner ring and a yellow outer ring. Four small moons orbit the planet: one yellow and three orange moons pocked with craters that make them look a little like oranges. A loud alarm and a flashing red light rudely awakens Uphrasia and Konrad from their sleep. In various ducts rats are hustling and bustling around in a frenzy of activity. Uphrasia and Konrad meet Thompus in the main junction and watch the chaos. Uphrasia puts his paw on Konrad's shoulder. "No volunteering, remember?" Konrad nods. Nute scurries along towards them carrying a box of gadgets and gizmos. Uphrasia grabs her arm. "What's all the commotion about Nute?"

Nute looks at him and her lens motors whirr as the lens moves back and forth. "Planet, exploration, volunteers, highly dangerous, got to go!" She pants twice and moves off down the duct then calls back. "Shuttle departing in five minutes!"

"A planet!"

Konrad's eyes bulge. "An eating opportunity!"

"We'll probably all die if we go there" remarks Thompus.

Rose steps out of a duct wearing a spacesuit.

"You're going?!" exclaims Uphrasia looking surprised.

She beams a wide smile. "Of course, wouldn't miss it for the world; or, for another world in this case."

He creases his snout. "Now if I don't go I'll look like a scaredy-rat."

Rose lowers her eyelids. "Scrod's offering double rations for all volunteers."

Konrad licks his lips. "We would be foolish not to go, foolish not to go!"

"I suppose you're right," sighs Uphrasia.

"What about all that stuff about not volunteering?" pleads Thompus.

Konrad drools. "Double rations – double rations!"

Uphrasia slaps him on the back. "OK we'll go. Just stop drooling."

"Sorry." He slurps and swallows.

Thompus makes a disgusted face. "You are truly repugnant."

"Thank you." Konrad grins.

In the huge cargo bay three space shuttles, short and square with pointed fronts, are parked. A few human technicians are milling around the bay busy refuelling and servicing the shuttles. Uphrasia,

Konrad, Rose, Thompus and Nute hide behind a stack of cargo boxes. They are all wearing spacesuits, have shiny new helmets under their arms and have their mission rucksacks on their backs. Scrod hops down from inside one of the landing gear compartments and whispers, "Plenty of room. In you go!" They all creep out, climb up the shuttle's landing gear, hop inside the cramped compartment and settle down.

Thompus looks around nervously. "Is this compartment airtight?"

"Helmets on!" orders Scrod as he enters.

They all attach their helmets as Professor Abler climbs in. "Sorry I'm late. Now, don't eat or drink anything until Nute has tested it for toxins! Good luck everyone, and let's all return safely." He squeezes in next to Nute and puts on his helmet. "Oh, and remember where they park the shuttlecraft."

Scout watches the shuttle as the engines roar. "Awe shucks, they get to go and visit a new world, while I have to complete this boring survey of the ship. Nothing exciting ever happens to me these days." There is a sudden white flash. A laser zaps him and he drops down unconscious. A Cybormoggy walks past him and climbs onto the shuttle's single forward leg just in time as the shuttle lifts up, blasts out of the cargo bay and arcs towards the planet. The landing gear legs start to rise up. The rats all pull their paws back as the landing gear enters the compartment. The front leg jams, sandwiching the Cybormoggy with a loud crunch. The shuttle darts past one of the orange moons then arcs downwards. It enters the atmosphere and the forward shield glows white hot with a halo of fire. It disappears in a cloud of yellow mist then re-emerges and cools as it descends towards the surface. The retro thrusters blast, slowing the shuttle down.

The planet is barren except for a few scrubby bushes with fluffy white buds on their skinny branches. The ground is rocky, yellow and very dusty. Here and there orange and yellow boulders sit in small craters. They have deep scars on their surfaces made by strong winds. Yellow and orange mountains fill the horizon with halos of orange and brown clouds against a deep blue sky. In the centre of these mountains the tallest has a deep volcanic crater. Black smoke rises up from it into the sky turning the yellow clouds brown where it meets them.

The shuttle extends its landing gear and touches down in a flat valley. Scrod is the first to hop out. "This way – follow me!" The rats hop out and head off together. The front half of the Cybormoggy drops onto the ground, rolls head over heels for a few feet then stops, smouldering and smoking. Its red eyes fade and go out.

The group wander about looking for signs of life as Abler fans an electronic device around. "The air quality seems fine, within safe parameters. Helmets off!" They all remove their helmets and breathe in.

Nute strokes her wires and frowns. She looks at Rose who returns an enquiring look. Nute shakes her head and Rose steps up close to her. "What is it?"

"Bad feeling."

"On the scale of one to ten? One, like we should be concerned or ten, like we should run around screaming?"

"Ten, like we should to go back to the shuttle right now."

"That's a very bad ten then."

Konrad scrunches up his snout. "Poo, what a pong! It's just like a rotten crow's egg!"

Professor Abler rubs some of the dust between his finger tips and sniffs it. "Sulphur, possibly from some volcanic activity."

As they climb down a steep slope into a valley, Nute picks a bud of fluff from a bush and places a sample in her toxin-testing unit. Abler looks at her over his spectacles. "Edible?"

She hums, staring at the screen of the unit and shakes her head. "Ah! Nobody eat the white fluff!"

Uphrasia holds a clump in his paw. "Why not? It looks quite harmless!"

"It has a mild sedative toxin that may cause drowsiness, even deep sleep."

The others gather round her and Thompus shakes his paw trying to shake off a blob of sticky fluff. "Good job you warned us in time."

Rose looks around. "Konrad, Konrad?!"

139

Uphrasia looks back. "He was right behind us."

"You three double back and look for him," orders Scrod. "We can't have anyone left behind."

Uphrasia, Rose and Thompus head back up the slope. At the top they find Konrad laying on his back snoring, white fluff all around his mouth.

Uphrasia tilts his head to one side. "No guessing what happened here then."

The ground starts to shake and they wobble around and Thompus yells through his chattering teeth "Whoa!"

Uphrasia grabs Rose's arms and they steady each other. "Tremor!" Rose yells as a cloud of yellow dust covers them.

The tremor subsides and the two let go of each other, embarrassed. Uphrasia pats the dust off his fur. "We should head back to the shuttle." He starts to pick up Konrad by the shoulders.

Rose frowns. "What about the others?"

"They know the rules, the Rat Way."

"No! We go back for Nute, the Professor and General Scrod. He said no one gets left behind! He gave us specific orders! I'm not budging on this, not this time!"

"OK, OK! It's very unorthodox but we'll go back."

She picks up one of Konrad's arms and Thompus takes his feet, moaning. "Why do I have to lug this dead weight!"

"You're one to talk!"

They reach the brow of the slope and find Scrod and Nute climbing up with Abler trailing behind. The ground shakes again and rocks start rolling and bouncing down the hill.

"Hurry!" shouts Uphrasia. Scrod grabs Nute's arm and helps her up the slope. Then a huge crevasse ruptures the valley below, molten lava erupts in a great curtain and jets up into the sky.

Thompus whines. "Great! Now a volcano. We've really had our chips!"

Scrod and Nute reach the top and the others pull them up onto the level. Scrod surveys the valley below. "Quickly! Back to the shuttle!" Abler finally joins them and they run on all fours. Smouldering rocks land on the ground and bounce around them. Konrad is still out cold as the other three carry him.

"Raining rocks! Why me?!" Thompus wails.

Scrod urges him on. "Keep moving!" They reach the valley where the shuttle landed only to see it lift off and blast up into the sky.

Nute's jaw drops. "No!"

"Were doomed!" Thompus puffs and sweats, hyperventilating. He does not notice a set of tracks like a line scraped in the ground right next to his feet.

Abler hobbles up puffing and gasping. "We need to find shelter immediately."

Scrod scours the hills and spots a dark shadow up on the side of the mountain. "A cave! We can shelter in there. Quick, everyone!"

They all run up the opposite slope and start to climb towards the cave entrance. Uphrasia huffs as he struggles with his end of Konrad, he looks back at Rose. "Are you OK?"

"What do you care, Mister I follow the Rat Way!" They scramble up towards the cave and drag Konrad inside.

Something watches them from behind a rock as Scrod hurries Nute up the hill, but Abler is ten metres or so behind. "Wait for Grandpa!"

Scrod's head darts around. "There's no time. Come on Professor!"

Abler struggles up the hill, waving them on and gasping for breath. "Go on, be safe my dear, I'll catch up." Thud! A huge molten rock hammers him into the ground.

Scrod turns Nute around. "Don't look!"

They run into the cave and stand looking out at the rocks and ash falling in the valley below.

"Professor Abler?" Enquires Rose. Scrod shakes his head. She spins around and vents her anger at Uphrasia, "Why didn't you go back for him?!"

Scrod holds up his paw to calm her. "It's not his fault, there was no time."

Nute walks over to the edge of the cave and sits down with her back to them. Rose lets loose. "You and your stupid Rat Way! Your selfishness has cost Professor Abler his life." She storms across the cave, sits next to Nute and puts her arm round her shoulders. She looks over her shoulder and scowls at Uphrasia.

He looks at the floor and spits, "Damn it!"

Thompus is resigned to his fate. "We're all going to die here, aren't we? I mean, if we're not burned to charcoal, we will never get off this forsaken rock!"

Scrod stands to attention. "Now, now! Let's have none of that quitting talk! We are rats, and what do we always do?"

"We survive." Thompus mumbles.

"That's right! We survive because of our selfishness, blind optimism and reckless boldness."

Nute sobs and Rose tries to console her. "Don't fret, Nute. We'll make it."

Nute lies down on her tummy. "I don't want to be a rat anymore." She buries her face in her folded arms.

Scrod looks out of the cave entrance and watches as clouds of yellow-and-black smoke rise up the slope towards them. "We must move away from the entrance!" Scrod takes a torch out of his rucksack and shines it deep into the dark depths of the cave. There is a small crack and he pokes his head through. "This will do. Come on all of you, quickly!" They all squeeze through the crack and enter a dark tunnel.

Out on the mountainside the remains of the Cybormoggy drags itself up towards the cave with a few wires trailing behind. It passes Abler's body then moves on up. At the cave entrance it scans for lifeforms, then for temperature fluctuations. On its internal viewer it sees a red glow where the warm bodies of the rats have been. The heat trails all lead to the crack in the wall where they glow more intensely orange and yellow.

The rats enter a great dark cavern. They take out their torches and switch them on as they walk along a narrow ledge. The beams of their torches light up tall rounded stalagmites rising up around them, and their opposites, stalactites, hanging down from the ceiling. Water drips from their tips onto the rat's heads and Srcod stops and opens his mouth to catch the refreshing drops. Steam vapour rises up from a pit that glows fiery red deep in the bowels of the mountain. Scrod looks down into it. "We better keep moving. I don't like the look of that!" They climb up a steep rise and find a hole that is lit from inside. Scrod pokes his head in. "It looks safe enough. Can't be sure." He enters first, wriggling through; then his head re-appears through the hole. "It's alright folks, come on inside." The inside of the small cave is covered in stunning amber-coloured crystals from floor to ceiling that glow with a warm golden light.

Nute forgets her emotions for a moment, mesmerised by the beauty of this natural light show.

"Calcite!" The others pull Konrad in through the hole and lay him down on the ground. They switch off their torches and look up. Rose touches the surface of the crystals.

"Where is the light coming from?"

"It glows with thermoluminescence, from the heat of the volcano. So beautiful!" Nute takes out her penknife and prises off some of the crystals.

Scrod looks up at the glowing ceiling. "I think we'll be safe here for a short while. Just until we figure out what to do next. Try to get some rest all of you."

The eruption has ceased. All is quiet. The rats lie fast asleep, huddled together on the cave floor. Konrad lays on his back snoring. Uphrasia gets up, sits down next to him and pushes him over onto his side. Konrad stops snoring and sleeps soundly. Although he can't hear a word, Uphrasia talks to him quietly. "You've been a loyal friend to me old pal, you put up with my moods and tantrums and you stuck by me." Uphrasia looks up at the glittering cave roof. "Our whole world seems to be changing so fast and I can't keep up with it. It's like everything I believed in is out dated, redundant. Am I rodundant?" He looks down and lets out a deep sigh. "Thanks for listening anyway buddy." He pats Konrad on the shoulder and lays down and goes to sleep.

Thompus mumbles in his sleep. "Good night, good night! Parting is such sweet sorrow."

The Cybormoggy crawls along the narrow ledge a few inches at a time. Its voice is feint and crackles. "Exterminate all vermin! Exterminate all vermin!" It digs its claws into the slippery ground and drags itself along.

A moonbeam enters through a tiny hole in the roof of the cave and moves slowly across the floor. Something stirs in the shadows. A white, glowing worm slithers out across the cave floor and over to where the rats are sleeping. It is very long and as thick as one of their snouts. It moves silently up to Rose's left foot then lifts its head up, opens its mouth and its whole face peels inside out and back along its body. It starts to roll its face over Rose's foot and up her leg. Very slowly it starts to drag Rose along the cave floor towards the darkness. The beam of light moves along the floor and lights up Konrad's face. He yawns, opens his eyes and sits up. "Wow! What a light show! Are we camping?!" He gets up, walks through the sleeping rats and steps on the worm which makes a squelching sound as green and yellow goo squashes out. It then shakes itself violently, unwraps itself from Rose's foot and silently slithers off back into the darkness. Konrad watches, bemused, then shrugs, sniffs the air and looks up to where the beam of light is coming from. He climbs up the wall of crystals, stands on a rocky ledge, sticks his head out through the hole and looks up into the starry sky. He scratches his groin, yawns and gazes up misty eyed at a bright light falling through the few wispy clouds. "I can see a falling star. It's beautiful!" The bright, glowing light leaves a burning white trail that fades as it descends toward the valley below. Konrad frowns. "Are comets meant to slow down?"

Scrod sits bolt upright. "What's that?!" He rapidly climbs up the wall, steps up beside Konrad and watches through the hole as the light gets closer. "A spaceship! Wake up, wake up everyone! There's a ship. We must stow away before it departs!" They all get on their feet, stretch and yawn. Nute takes a pawful of the crystals and puts them in her rucksack. Then another white worm appears over her head. Again the mouth peels back around its body then suddenly it darts forward and grabs her by the shoulder. Nute screams and Uphrasia dashes over and tries to pull the squirming worm off. Three more worms slither over a tall, black and very smooth rock, down towards them. They take out their torches and swipe them away. One worm snatches and gulps down Thompus' torch and the light slides along the worm's stomach, lighting it up with a dull glow from inside as it goes back over the rock. More worms appear, slithering over the rock. They seem to be very long as their back ends trail off into the darkness. On top of the rock a huge figure appears. A giant slimy megoroslug monster lets out a huge roar! The worms are long tentacles attached to its mouth, and two great big, hungry black eyes on stalks stare down at them. The rats back up as the megoroslug slithers over the rock. It attaches another tentacle to Nute and starts to lift her up towards its open mouth, a circle of sharp, triangular, blade-like teeth start gnashing and grinding. "Help me!" Nute cries. Rose ducks as a tentacle darts at her. It misses, striking the wall of crystals behind her. There is a loud hiss and the tentacle zips back behind the black rock. Rose looks back over her shoulder to see a blob of slime smoking on the crystals. She leans down and picks up a pawful of crystal gravel and throws it as hard as she can at the mouth of the nearest tentacle. It swallows the grit and is frozen for a moment. Then it lets out a huge sneeze and explodes, splattering green and orange goo all over the cavern. Uphrasia leaps up and grabs Nute by the feet and hangs on to her. The tentacles pull her closer and closer to the gnashing teeth and Uphrasia braces his legs against the rock and tugs back on Nute. "Ouch you're stretching me!"

Scrod and Konrad hop down and Rose gives them a pawful of grit each. "The monster seems to be harmed by the crystals! Aim for the mouth!" They all start to throw pawfuls of crystals at the beast, but they are too far away to get any in the mouth. A long tentacle wraps itself round and round Thompus, slowly turns him on his side and lifts him towards the monster's mouth, head first.

"Yikes it's going to gobble me up! Do something, please!?" His head is inches from the mouth of the megoroslug and the teeth gnash and grind faster and faster. Clear, gooey drool drips onto Thompus' face as he wriggles and squirms!

Konrad picks up a large crystal in both paws. "Make a stack!"

Rose looks at Scrod. "There's only two of us!"

"That will do!"

Uphrasia hangs onto Nute's legs straining against the pull of the megoroslug's tentacle. Nute cries out, "Ouch! Help!"

Scrod crouches down and Rose hops onto his shoulders. Konrad squats then runs forward and leaps up, his right foot landing on Scrod's back and his left on Rose's shoulder. He flies through the air holding the crystal out and lands head first in the mouth of the megoroslug. The teeth stop gnashing, the giant black eyes move slowly down to look at Konrad's back end and tail sticking out of its mouth. Then it grunts, gags once, grunts twice, then kaboom!!! The whole body of the megoroslug explodes in a giant mass of slime and sticky goo! All the rats land on the ground covered in sluggy-entrails.

Konrad lands on his back with a big splat in a giant gooey puddle. Nute sits up in a layer of slime. She wipes her face and eyes and looks at Konrad. "Thanks! I think."

"Welcome."

The others get up and brush off the slime. Scrod is covered from head to toe in the thickest layer of goo. He shakes himself free and wipes his face. "Yuck! What a fiendish beast. Tastes like slug! It must have mutated! I wonder how on earth it got here?" Konrad takes out his penknife and slices a large chunk of tentacle off and stuffs it into his rucksack.

Nute shakes her torch and it flickers to life. "I for one will never eat slug again! Or worms too come to think of it!" Her torchlight momentarily catches something moving in the dark depths of the cavern. She points the torch back at it. "Guys!" They all turn on their torches and point them into the darkness. Everywhere the torchlights land they see more and more megoroslugs slithering slowly towards them.

"We better get the hell out of here! Rats on the double! Up here!" They all start to climb up the cave wall towards the small hole. The Cybormoggy arrives, the hatch on its head opens, the laser weapon rises up and it targets Thompus. On its internal view screen the crosshairs lock on to him as he climbs the cave wall. "Exterminate all vermin! Exterminate all vermin!" It fires but the weapon just sparks and makes a fizzing sound. Konrad squeezes out first, followed by Nute, Rose, Uphrasia and Thompus, then finally by Scrod. Three slug tentacles reach out of the hole after them but they hop clear and clamber down onto a rocky plateau. They look down onto the flat plain below. The ship floats down towards the valley and they can just hear the roar of the retro rockets as it slows down to land. The rats race down the slope onto the plain. The Cybormoggy crawls along the floor of the cave. "Destroy all vermin!" A tentacle lands on its back, lifts it up and carries it to the gnashing teeth of a megoroslug's mouth. "Destroy! Destroy!" There is a loud crunch and the Megoroslug swallows the Cybormoggy.

They all walk down the steep slope towards the plain. The volcanic activity has stopped and black smoke rises from a deep trench. Nute slows down as she passes Abler's crushed body. Only his pink tail is poking out from under the giant smouldering boulder. She frowns, stifles a tear and whispers, "Grandpa." Scrod guides her past.

# Chapter 9
## FLUFF TIME

As the Vandal touches down steam and gas exit the exhaust vents. A gangway lowers and the Bilothian crew drive out of the cargo hold on three brightly coloured dune buggies with headlights blazing at the front. They park side by side, in a straight line. Each buggy has been customised to suit the driver. Gark and Tark's buggy is decorated with black and white stripes. Gark sits at the front and Tark sits facing backwards in a rear seat. A large cannon sits on the back end and Tark polishes the bright-green barrel. "It is my turn at the front, we agreed last time!"

Gark cranes around. "We did not agree anything! You said you like the back because you like to shoot the weapon!"

"I like the weapon but I would prefer to be at the front!"

Gark shakes his head exasperated. "There is just no pleasing some folk."

Carak sits in his white-and-orange buggy which has two huge bumpers front and back while Spigot revs the engine of his yellow buggy with bright green dots all over it. It has a tall spindle in the middle with a propeller at the top. Bibulous walks down the gangway and stops at the bottom. "Pay attention! Do not eat any fluff until you are back here and are off duty. Punishment will be severe if you fail to obey!"

They all moan and groan.

"Silence! Fetch the supplies and be back here before sunset. I want to get off this stinking planet!"

Carak raises his hand.

"What is it Carak?!"

"Count us down boss."

"What?! No! You're not racing today!" They all stare at him. "Forget it, I'm not playing this game with you!" None of them move, they just stare at him until finally he rolls his eyes. "Three, two, one. Go!" Carak's foot hits the peddle, the back wheels spin and he darts off. Spigot races off after him. Gark and Tark are still arguing.

Tark shakes his fist. "Accelerate! Idiot!"

"I am accelerating moron! You have your foot on the brake!"

Tark looks down. "Oh!" He lifts his foot and they dart off swerving all over the place.

Bibulous shakes his head. "Morons!" He covers his left and right eyes with his hands and his antenna lowers to cover his middle eye. Then he lowers his arms, turns and walks back up the gangway. "I'm surrounded by morons!"

The rats watch from behind a rock. Scrod creeps out, tiptoes towards the alien ship and peeks up the gangway. He sniffs the air then beckons them over. They all trot up the gangway into the cargo hold.

A few scattered crates and tool stations give them cover as they tiptoe across and creep through an open hatch at the far side and enter a short corridor with two hatches on each side and an open hatch at the end.

Bibulous sits in his big comfy command chair on the bridge with his feet up, scrolling through star charts on the big screen. A number of planets appear. "Too small, too far away, too fat. Asteroids! Boring..." The planet Earth appears on the screen. "Hmm, didn't we blow that one up last week?"

In the background, one by one, the rats tiptoe across the room. Scrod takes a tool from his utility belt and unscrews the bolts holding an air vent in place close to the floor. Then, they all squeeze inside except Nute who stops to look around at all the flickering lights and bright consoles, eyes wide, she whispers, "Oh!!"

Uphrasia beckons her from an air vent. "Nute. Nute come on." She stops by Carak's weapon station, and open mouthed she admires the hi-tech console, the flashing lights and information screens.

Bibulous continues to search, then he stops abruptly. "Huh!" His wonky antenna starts to wobble and wave around. He spins round in his chair and scours the room behind him. Nute is hiding behind a metal ceiling support, making herself very thin. Bibulous' three huge bulging eyes narrow, scanning left and right. "Humph!" He turns back to the view screen.

Nute hops into the duct and the others breathe a sigh of relief. Scrod gathers them round and whispers, "I suggest we all keep our heads down until we can work out what kind of creatures these are."

The other Bilothians race each other across the plain. Carak is in front closely followed by Gark and Tark. Spigot has his head down and drives up close behind Gark and Tark. He pulls out and accelerates and starts to overtake. Tark grins at him and points his cannon at his face. Spigot looks right just as Tark pulls the trigger and a great jet of orange gunge flies out of the canon and hits Spigot in the face with a splat! Spigot weaves about, slams his foot on the brakes and stops in a cloud of dust. Tark hoots and giggles. "Got you bang smack in the chops! He, he!" Gark hits the accelerator and rams Carak from behind. Carak narrows his eyes, lowers his head and accelerates. He approaches a group of stubby trees with low branches on each side of the track. Carak pulls a lever and a door opens at the back of his buggy revealing a small cannon. As he drives through the trees he presses a button and a net is fired out of the cannon. It spreads out and lands suspended between the branches by tiny hooks. Gark is hot on his heels and hits the net. It stretches, then he is lifted out of the buggy and catapulted back along the track. Carak hoots with laughter as Gark bounces head over heels on the dusty plain behind him, tangled up in the net. Tark looks confused as the buggy weaves off the track, up a steep slope where it pauses for a moment then flips back and lands on top of him with a crash. Carak takes out a net on a short pole. Then as he drives past some low shrubs he reaches out the net and captures big clumps of fluff with it. He is about to take a mouthful when a shadow floats over him. He looks up to see Spigot hovering above with his propeller spinning and pulsing. There is a large yellow rock suspended on a cable beneath his buggy. Spigot laughs an evil laugh, "He, he, he!" He pulls a lever and the rock falls landing on the bonnet of Carak's buggy. It flips over sending Carak flying through the air. He crashes into the thick thicket of fluff bushes. "Ha, ha, ha! Get some fluff Carak! Wahoo!" Spigot is so busy gloating he crashes straight into a tall, pointy orange rock and slides down landing in a heap at the bottom. Tark and Gark's heavily dented buggy limps along, missing one back wheel. They pull up next to Spigot as he crawls out of his wrecked buggy. Spigot looks up to see Tark looking down his cannon barrel at him. SPLAT! A huge glob of gunge hits him in the face. "Ha... Ha...," mocks Tark.

Gark shakes his head in disapproval. "Cold, you're cold."

Tark takes offence. "I am not! It was an 'in the heat of the moment' thing."

"I say you're a cold ruthless being!"

"Well lahdi dah! Look who's talking!"

Bibulous is still hunting for a target when an image of the Patrick Moore appears on his view screen. He sits upright and zooms in. "Aha! Lots of advanced lifeforms. Plenty of salvage to steal. Flammable fuel source and a nuclear power plant to boot. Should make a splendid explosion!" The sound of engines distracts him; he switches off the view screen, gets up and waddles through the corridor, out into the cargo hold and down the gangway. The other Bilothians have returned. Gark and Tark tow Spigot's wreck with him sitting on top of it. Carak is covered in tiny scratches as he drives his buggy home. They all sing at the top of their voices. "Fluff, fluff, fluff! We love fluff!"

"Get a move on! You befuddled nincompoops!" As they all drive up the gangway Carak drives over Bibulous' foot. "Ooh, oh, oh!" Bibulous hops about, holding his bruised big toe. "Carak you bumbling buffoon!"

On the bridge, Bibulous, his right foot bandaged, waits hands on hips as the others file in holding little leather bags bulging with fluff. "Carak! Did you get the water?"

"No Captain. The lake was dry. This planet is finished boss."

Bibulous takes their bags of fluff and locks them in his locker. "There now. You can have your rations when we have destroyed this planet and are on our break!" They all grumble and moan. "To your posts you mutinous dogs!" he orders wearily. They scatter to their work stations and Bibulous hobbles over to his command chair, lifts his foot onto his console and rests it on a thick fluffy cushion. "Ouch, oh, oh!"

With a mighty roar white fire blasts out of the engines at the back of the ship. The landing gear retracts as jets of fire blast down from the underside. It rises in a cloud of orange dust and blasts up into the sky. The Vandal breaks free of the atmosphere, then rapidly moves away from the planet until it is just a tiny speck on the view screen. Then it slows and turns around a hundred and eighty degrees. The crew wait silently for instruction, hands hovering over their controls. Bibulous takes a deep breath and speaks in a rather bored tone. "And... Activate the Obliterator."

Carak flicks the switch. "Obliterator activated and in position!"

"Charge the Obliterator." He waves his hand in a circle in the air.

"Charging the Obliterator!" With a wide grin Carak presses another button and pulls down the big lever.

Bibulous operates a joystick on his panel, and a crosshair darts about his screen over the planet. "Targeting planet! Locked on – fire when ready."

Carak watches the needle on the gauge move slowly from left to right and into the red, then he slams his fist on the large red fire button. "Fire!"

The laser fires and fans out towards the planet, which burns in a giant ball of fire and then explodes into a cloud of yellow and orange light. Then it implodes with a loud pop! Then, BOOM! Two circular shockwaves blast out into space. The Vandal spins round and round in their wake. The bridge shakes and they all hang on until it settles. Then, they cheer and laugh.

Carak hops up and down excitedly. "Fluff time!"

Bibulous frowns. "Fluff time!? Do you really think you deserve any fluff after what you did to my foot?"

Carak gulps and looks at him with three wide, innocent eyes. "Probably?"

Bibulous scowls at him, then he smiles, if you can call it a smile, as all his teeth are so yellow and very, very pointy it looks more like a fierce growl. "Very well. Since I am feeling generous today I will let you each have half of a ration! I will consume the rest myself." They all moan as he unlocks the cupboard and hands out their bags. "After our nap we have something very special to destroy."

Carak can't contain his enthusiasm. "What is it? What is it?!"

"Ah, ah! I don't want to spoil the surprise." Bibulous waves his finger left and right.

Gark looks at Tark's bag of fluff. "You have more than me!"

"We have exactly the same amount."

"Once again you ignore my needs for your own selfish ends."

"What is wrong with you today? All you do is complain!"

Bibulous holds up both his hands above his head. "Will you both just stop arguing and go and eat your fluff!"

They both walk over to their post. Gark says under his breath. "Selfish. So selfish."

"I'm not sharing with you if that's what you think."

"You see? Selfish."

They all sit down, stuffing large clumps of the fluff into their huge mouths and one by one fall fast asleep at their stations. Bibulous pulls a lever and a metal bunk drops down. He rolls into it and stuffs a gigantic clump of fluff into his enormous wide mouth. He munches and swallows. "Ah. Peace at last." Then he closes his three big round eyes. Then he opens his left eye, looks left and right, then closes it again.

Scrod furtively pokes his head out of the duct. "Come on!" They all enter the bridge as Scrod paces up and down. "This is a dreadful situation, really dreadful! These monsters can't be allowed to go around just blowing up planets, willy-nilly! I mean, how will we find our new home?"

Nute climbs up on the captain's chair and inspects the control panel. She presses a button and the screen comes to life.

"Nute, be careful what you touch!" Scrod warns.

"The technology of this ship is highly advanced. Oh no!" On the screen is an image of the Patrick Moore. "They're going to destroy our ship, all our friends!"

Scrod marches over. "Nonsense. Let me see." He squints up at the screen. "It seems the brainy one is right."

Nute hops down from the chair. "We can't let them destroy our ship, can we?"

Scrod punches one paw into the palm of the other. "I'm torn. The Rat Way states clearly it's every rat for himself. It's a rule we have all lived and prospered by for thousands of years. Do you seriously expect me to turn my back on all that history and risk everything to save a few hundred rats and a loathsome human crew?"

Tears well up in Nute's eyes. "Yes." She stares at him with the saddest, most desperate look a rat can manage.

"Don't look at me like that; I can't think dispassionately!"

Rose interjects. "She's right! We have to help our friends, it's in all our best interests to get back on the Patrick Moore."

Uphrasia throws open his arms. "Here she goes again! Look, the humans killed my mother. They are our sworn enemy. They would kill us as soon as look at us. Remember the Cybormoggy, the way they tortured Thompus?

"The food wasn't bad." Thompus remarks.

Uphrasia holds up his paws. "We hate them!"

Rose puts her paws on his shoulders. "If you feel so bad about your past, how bad will you feel in the future if you don't make things right? Right now!"

He pulls away. "Now you're starting to sound like Konrad! I'm confused."

"I have to agree with Rose", pipes up Thompus. "After all, there are a lot of ship's stores to get through on our ship. I'm all for going back."

Uphrasia paces up and down. "Nonsense! We hide here and wait until we find a safe place to hop off. It's the Rat Way: every rat for himself. Right, Konrad?"

Konrad looks at his feet. "I don't feel right in my tummy."

Carak mumbles in his sleep and rolls over. Scrod ushers them back towards the vent. "Quickly! There's no time to debate this now. Everyone back in the duct!" They all enter the vent and Scrod stands guard just inside, pulling the grill closed he watches through the slits.

The Bilothian crew start to stir and stretch. Bibulous wakes up and hops down from his bunk, forgetting his sore foot. "Ouch!" He hops over to his command console. "Ooh, ooh!" Then he looks up at the screen where the image of the Patrick Moore is displayed. His face changes to a sour scowl and he slowly turns and looks at each member of the crew one by one. In a sinister voice he asks "Who peeked?!"

The other Bilothians groan and stretch as they wake. They look at each other wondering who did it. Carak defends, "We've been asleep all the time your great voluminousness."

Tark points at Gark. "It was him!"

"Liar! It was not me! It was probably you! Buck passer!"

"One of you looked at my surprise! If there is one thing I can't stand it is a sneak. No, wait. I like sneaks. Either way, someone is getting punished. Bring me the Electrocutor!" Bibulous holds out his hand, palm open.

Spigot opens a cupboard and takes out a white rod with a short handle. He looks dejected as he is about to hand it over when Bibulous holds up his hand. "Wait!" His antenna wiggles and wobbles again. He looks up at it and frowns. He sniffs, crosses the room, sniffs again. "If I am not mistaken we have an intruder aboard! It seems I may have misjudged you all. Shame, I was looking forward to torturing you." Spigot lets out a long sigh of relief. Bibulous approaches the duct and notices the bolts have been undone. His three large eyes widen. "My antenna is never wrong!"

Scrod looks at the other rats, then back out at Bibulous as he gets closer to the duct, he whispers. "Get yourselves to a safe hiding place! I'll take care of this." They all move out of sight around a bend in the duct as Scrod kicks open the vent, leaps out and knocks Bibulous on his back. Bibulous thumps and kicks. Scrod bites his bandaged foot.

Bibulous yells out in pain. "Argh!! He kicks Scrod back hard with his good foot, gets up and hops about. "Attack the intruder!" Scrod is about to counter attack, when BUZZ! All his hair stands on end and he flops onto the floor, out cold. Spigot stands behind him grinning with the smoking Electrocutor rod in hand.

Bibulous hops over to the vent, yanks it open and peers in. The duct is empty.

Carak pulls Scrod along the deck by his feet. "Shall I shoot this intruder out into space captain?"

"Yes! Blast it out into the vacuum of space and let's watch it die of asphyxiation!" Carak drags Scrod out into the corridor and hits a button next to the hatch on the left and the air lock door slides open. He pushes Scrod into the air lock and closes the hatch, then reaches for the lever to open the external hatch.

"Wait!" Bibulous bellows. "We have to stop for water on the next planet. We can drop this stowaway off there, then obliterate the planet and fry him in the process!"

"Evil genius master; you truly are a most rotten individual."

Bibulous grins. "Yes, I am rather pleased with myself for my brilliance, charm and vile imagination. Now. I want to blow up that spaceship! We will get fresh water supplies first. Set a course for planet P373B. I like the tasty purple fruit there. Let's go, Bilothians!" His crew busy themselves at their posts. Carak opens the hatch and ties Scrod up tightly with a rope.

Gark operates his half of the console and Tark barges him with his shoulder. "Why don't you ever come up with any good ideas like that?"

Gark looks offended. "I have ideas."

"Huh! Like what?"

"Gark pulls down a large lever in front of Tark's face. "I was the one who discovered the fluff!"

"Oh come on! Fluff grows on over seventy planets in this galaxy!"

"Well I discovered it on this particular planet."

In a grubby hanger full of garbage, broken equipment and rotting food, a small vent opens and the five remaining rats climb out. They find a small space in the garbage and huddle together. Konrad licks a red-and-blue vegetable. "Yuk! Tastes like a cat's armpit."

"What will we do without General Scrod?" whines Nute.

Rose announces in a confident tone, "I say we formulate a plan to defeat the aliens, communicate with the humans, then get back on board our ship. Simple!"

Uphrasia raises his eyebrows. "And just tell me how we go about defeating five, large, hostile aliens?"

She folds her arms. "Well, I haven't worked out that part of our plan yet."

"Right, then. We hide here and wait until it's all over, OK?"

Thompus' eyes bulge. "Wait! Communicate with the humans! I can do that! I can type a message. If only we can find a way to send it."

"You can type a message to the humans? Uphrasia looks doubtful."

"Yes – yes, I can." He taps his dome with his forefinger. "If we can download their ship's operation manual into my memory chip I think I can manage to send a message."

Rose claps her paws. "All we need now is some communications access."

Nute frowns. "Well, I suppose I could operate their communications system."

Uphrasia shakes his head, exasperated. "We don't have time. We're not trained to take on such a dangerous mission and we are outsized and outnumbered!"

Rose folds her arms and scowls at him. "Scrod sacrificed himself for us. You can stay here and hide like a little kit, or you can come along with us and try to help!"

"You could lead us, be a hero!" Nute encourages.

"I'm not the hero type!"

"Be not afraid of greatness. Some are born great, some achieve greatness, and some have greatness thrust upon 'em." Thompus grins.

Uphrasia turns his back to them. "Konrad and I will stay here!"

Konrad looks confused and torn, he looks at Rose who nods encouragement. "Konrad?"

The poor little chap looks at his feet, forlorn. "I'm sorry, guys." He steps up next to Uphrasia.

"Very well. We will do it without you!" Rose and the other two start to head back to the bridge, then they all start to slide across the floor as the room tips up. They all cling onto each other. Konrad's feet skitter on the slippery surface. "Yikes!" A huge pile of food and garbage falls on top of them and they are pushed towards the back wall.

Nute grabs hold of Konrad's tail and clings on. "What's happening?!"

The Vandal is plummeting through the atmosphere of planet P373B which is lush and green. It slows down, extends its landing gear, and lands in a beautiful green meadow full of flowers and trees in full blossom. At the back of the ship, a wide hatch opens and with a loud farting noise a huge cube of stinking garbage drops out and lands with a thud on the ground. The rats, who are firmly stuck in the cube, wriggle and struggle out. Konrad is upside down and at the top of the cube, heaves his upper half out. "Argh that was a smelly squash!" He drops to the ground and they all race over to a thick line of thorny bushes just in time as the gangway of the Vandal lowers. Carak and Spigot exit carrying water cans, and Gark and Tark carry Scrod tied up with rope and hanging from a long pole between them. Rose scowls at Uphrasia. "They have General Scrod. I suppose we leave him to his fate. Is that your plan?"

"Well I suppose we could follow and see what they are up to." The rats creep along through the undergrowth then slither through a grassy meadow in single file. The Bilothians reach a circle of trees and drop Scrod on the ground then march off.

Rose tries to peer over Uphrasia's head. "I can't see! The grass is too high. We better stack up." Uphrasia and Thompus crouch on all fours. Rose and Nute hop on top of them and Konrad climbs up on the very top of the stack.

Thompus grumbles under the weight. "Ooh! How come the heavy one is on top?"

Konrad's sharp little eyes dart about. "The aliens have gone. General Scrod is tied up. There is a lovely tree with purple flowers." The stack collapses and Konrad bounces onto the ground. "Hey!"

They burst out into the meadow and gather round Scrod. Nute gently strokes his head. "Please don't be dead!"

Scrod has his eyes tightly shut. "If any of you ever mention this I'll court-martial the lot of you!"

Nute dives on him, hugs and kisses him. "You're alive! You're alive!"

"OK, enough hugging and kissing! Untie me quick!" Konrad nibbles the rope with his sharp front teeth and they release him. "This planet has potential. We should take a look around."

"What about the alien ship? Shouldn't we get back to it?" protests Rose.

"First we need food and water, then we need a first-rate plan. Come on!" He marches off.

"Does he even know where he's going?"

At the brow of a hill they pause and look down into a lush green valley with hundreds of fruit trees, flowers and short shrubs. Konrad stares, amazed. "It's Ratopia!" They race down the hill to a stream and all lay down and take a long drink of the crystal clear water. Konrad jumps in and splashes around, ducking his head and washing behind his ears.

Scrod sniffs the air. "Hmm... Something smells good. I'll scout up ahead. You lot scout around this area then return to rendezvous here." He disappears into a field of tall maize-like plants with bright red cobs. The others all wash off the smell of garbage then spread out and scout around. Konrad walks through a meadow filled with waste-high grass and pink flowers. He picks one of the flowers and takes a long sniff of the scent. Ten minutes later Uphrasia arrives in the same meadow and notices Konrad standing in the middle. "Konrad!" Konrad does not react. "Konrad!" He still does not respond. Uphrasia frowns and trots down the slope into the meadow. He steps on something and looks down. An alien skeleton is laying on the ground clutching a dried flower. It has a long domed head and a curved back. When he arrives he finds Konrad standing in a daze still holding the flower. Uphrasia pokes him and Konrad slowly turns and looks at him, holds up the flower and smiles. "Such a lovely scent." Uphrasia leans down and smells the flower.

Rose paces back and forth impatiently at the rendezvous point. "What is taking them so long?" She walks out onto the top of the meadow to see Uphrasia, Konrad, Nute and Thompus all standing in the middle of the meadow. "Hey guys!" None of them respond. She trots down the meadow towards them. There is a crack under her foot and she looks down to see the same alien skeleton holding a dried flower. Then another and another. There are hundreds of withered skeletons strewn across the field. She reaches the others and they all stand looking dazed.

"Hey guys, what happened to meeting up at the rendezvous point?"

Uphrasia holds up a flower. "Such a lovely scent." Rose notices that they are all holding the same flowers. She takes a step back. "Uphrasia!" He lifts the flower to his nose. Rose hops forward, snatches it and throws it down, then she takes the flowers out of the others' paws. She shakes Uphrasia by the shoulders. "Snap out of it Uphrasia, remember our mission!"

"Mission?"

Konrad leans down to pick another flower. "No!" Rose grabs him. "Konrad no flowers! All of you back up to the rendezvous point!" One by one she turns them to face back up the hill and ushers them forward. Nute picks a flower and Rose quickly takes it from her. "No! No flower picking!"

"Such a lovely scent," Nute protests.

Rose finally manages to get them all back to the tree by the stream and splashes water on their faces. They all slowly snap out of their dazed state.

Uphrasia scratches his tuft and yawns. "What's going on? Why are we here? Who am I?"

Rose looks directly in his face. "You're Private Teach of Space Corps, remember?" She slaps his face gently a few times. "Uphrasia!"

"Space Corps, ship's biscuits, remember?" His eyes open wide. "We were scouting."

"That's right, you were smelling the flowers and you forgot everything."

After about half an hour they all remember who they are and what had happened. They sit under a fruit tree in the warm sunshine waiting for Scrod to return. Konrad dozes when a large soft fruit drops onto his tummy, bounces off and lands on the ground. He picks it up and smells it.

"Wait!" Nute fumbles for her toxicology machine as Konrad's open jaw freezes, with the fruit held between his fingertips. "It may be toxic!" Saliva drips from Konrad's mouth, he sweats and his brow creases up. "I have to test it first!"

Uphrasia pleads with him. "Don't do it Konrad. Remember the fluff!" But it's too much for him to resist. He takes a bite of the fruit, chews and swallows.

Rose can't believe her eyes. "Are you crazy?!"

He licks his fingers. "The Rat Way states: eat first, and if you die don't eat it again. It's yummy!" He burps. "A bit fizzy though." He picks up another, tosses it into the air and swallows it whole.

Nute picks up one of the fruits, smells it and licks it. "It's fermented into alcohol."

Konrad is already eating another. "Zshish ones vewy nishe too. Hic!" In the background, Thompus burps.

"Not you, too?" Nute tests the fruit with her machine. "It seems OK."

Thompus holds a fruit between his thumb and forefinger. "He's right. They are jolly tasty; sweet with just a hint of sharpness."

Nute frowns, then nibbles the fruit. She rocks her head from side to side, making her wires rattle together, then takes a big bite. "Yum!"

Scrod walks through the vast field of tall, red maize. He sweats and wipes his brow and after a while reaches the end of the field. He parts the maize stalks and pokes his head through. A group of three roughly made straw huts cluster around a wicker food store. Three little reptilian aliens sit next to it. They have soft purple fur all over their bodies except for their heads and their hands which have large sharp claws. Their long mouths have fine, sharp little teeth and their two eyes are set into small domes that move around independently of each other. There is a ridge all the way along their backs leading down to a long scaly tail. They go about their business separating maize from the cob, mashing grain, kneading dough and making bread. They chatter together, absorbed in their work, making chirpy, bird-like sounds. These are the Tingoils, the renowned intergalactic space engineers.

Rose stands under the fruit tree with her arms folded. The other four roll around on the ground drunk. Konrad throws a pawful of mushy fruit at Thompus and it lands on his face and slides down leaving a purple stain. They all start throwing fruit.

Rose tries to stop them. "Guys, cut this out! What will General Scrod say?!" A large clump of mush hits her in the face. Furious she wipes it off. "Right!" She picks up a huge pile of fruit with both paws, squishes it together into a ball and throws it with all her might at Uphrasia who ducks just as Scrod parts the maize. The fruit hits him square in the face with a big SPLAT!

He shakes it off. "What's the meaning of this?!"

Konrad slurs. "Showy, we didn't know it wash contaminated sir. Hic!"

"Pull yourselves together and come with me!" Scrod barks. Then he vanishes into the maize. They all brush themselves down and follow. Rose hangs back as Uphrasia parts the maize and is about to enter.

"Uphrasia?!" Rose says in a sweet voice. He looks back just as a huge pile of mushy fruit hits him in the face. Rose doubles over laughing.

Uphrasia looks angry, then bursts out laughing. "OK I deserved that one."

Scrod shouts from a distance away, "Don't dilly dally!" The rats wander into the settlement and the Tingoils stop what they are doing and huddle together looking very afraid. Thompus and Konrad pull a woven straw lid off the food store and peek inside.

"Jackpot!" Thompus gasps, and they both tip their heads into the food store, pull out crude loaves of bread and start to scoff them down.

Scrod enters the nearest hut then comes out with a large pie containing purple fruit. He takes a huge bite and licks his lips. "Delicious! These chaps can really cook!"

Rose folds her arms, the corners of her mouth turning down. Uphrasia stands watching, beads of sweat roll down his snout. Konrad moves around the top of the food store. "Look, there's more over here!"

"Stop!" Snaps Uphrasia. They freeze and look at him in astonishment. Uphrasia marches forward. "Put it back!"

Konrad swallows a mouthful with a loud gulp. "Put it back? But what about the Rat Way?"

"Stuff the Way! Put it back, all of it!"

They reluctantly put back the food. Uphrasia looks over at Scrod, who hides the last piece of pie behind his back. Uphrasia scowls at him. "All of it!" Scrod tosses the pie back into the hut.

Thompus waves a crust of bread about in protest. "What's the problem here? It's just a few morsels of food."

Rose steps up next to Uphrasia. "It's not ours to take."

Uphrasia clears his throat. "Rose is right. We can't just take what we want, eat what we want and sleep where we want! We have to share, and, well, be nice to people and stuff."

Rose grins at him. "Great speech Churchill."

"Thanks, I was working on it all afternoon."

Scrod walks over and squares up to Uphrasia. "Now listen here, young rat! Our selfish Way has served us well for thousands of years and we have flourished as a species. The most successful mammal on Earth, after humans! Millions of us have been stealing, nipping peoples fingers and sleeping where we like!"

"Yes, but at what cost? Look where it's got us. Hated and feared by humans and just about every other species in the universe. If we take their food we're just as bad as those Vandals who destroy planets for no other reason but their sick amusement! We should be better than that!" He paces back and forth. "We should write a new Rat Way that is fair for everyone. We should be like, Gorgonzola!"

Scrod snorts. "Gorgonzola! Ha! It's a bedtime story made up by mothers to teach their children to behave. You can't expect us to change our ways because of a fantasy tale. I suppose you think we should help these pathetic little creatures as well?!"

"Now you mention it, yes!"

Rose kneels down before the Tingoils and reaches out her paw. "Don't be afraid, we mean you no harm."

Konrad walks over to them concealing a crust of bread behind his back. "I'm sorry little guys." He gives the nearest one the crust and a small scaly claw reaches out and takes it.

Scrod marches around in circles waving his arms about. "This is ridiculous. It goes against the grain! Being nice to people, not biting and stealing!" A shudder runs down his spine. "Ooh…" He shakes his arms.

Konrad's beady eyes twinkle. "It's not so bad, actually. I've got a warm, fuzzy feeling in my tummy. You ought to try it General."

Scrod straightens his back and folds his arms. "Humph! I couldn't, could I?" Then he steps forward and juts out his right paw towards one of the Tingoils. "General Scrod, Space Corps! Pleased to make your acquaintance."

A small shaking claw reaches out and takes his. "Fazool…"

Scrod's eyebrows raise and he gently shakes Fazool's claw. Another Tingoil holds out a loaf of bread, offering it to him. "Kazouri…"

"Huh!" He takes the bread. "No one has ever given me anything before. Not without a fight or at least a nip or two." Scrod spins around, gulps and stifles a tear. "I'll just patrol the perimeter." He marches off.

Konrad hops around grinning. "This is fantastic! We can live here with them in paradise!" Thompus joins him and they link arms and dance around in circles and sing together.

*"It's tough at the bottom of the food chain, when every day is do or die, and whenever you look up all you see is someone's..."*

"Guys stop – stop!" Uphrasia waves his paws up and down and they stop dancing.

Konrad frowns and wrinkles his snout as he always does when he's confused. "Now what? We're being nice now. I get it."

Uphrasia takes in a deep breath. "We're going back!"

Thompus looks shocked. "Back? Back where?"

Uphrasia starts pacing around the group. "Back to the alien spaceship, back to defeat the aliens and rescue the Patrick Moore. Back to being heroes!"

Thompus panics. "We don't have to die, we can stay here and live the good life here in Ratopia! Come on guys forget the Patrick Moore and those rotten humans! Forget danger and being heroes! We have everything we need right here! After all it sounds rather dangerous!"

Uphrasia looks at Rose and she nods in agreement. "We can't stay here. Those evil aliens will destroy this planet like they did the last one. So you see, either way we are destined to face danger and death."

Nute sighs. "Great, that's cheered me right up."

Rose puts her paw on Nute's shoulder and addresses them all in a serious tone, "We have got to defeat those aliens, warn the humans and save our friends! Our own survival depends on it."

Scrod appears beside her, puffs up his chest and clears his throat. "That's right. My plan of action is attack!" Now he is all fired up. "We overpower those evil aliens in mortal combat! Warn the humans of their impending destruction and rescue our shipmates! Who's with me?!" He holds out his paw in a fist looking left and right expectantly. "Anyone?"

Rose rolls her eyes. "Wow, what a fantastic plan! Where did it come from, I wonder?" She slams her paw on top of his. "I'm in!"

Nute hops forward and adds her paw. "Me too!"

Uphrasia slaps his paw down triumphantly. "Let's do this!"

Konrad shrugs and adds his paw. "OK I'll join the party!"

A Tingoil claw slaps down. "Fazool!"

Then another. "Kazouri!"

Then the third. "Metnaz!"

Thompus folds his arms and sulks, kicks a stone, looks at the ground and huffs. "I've had rocks fall on my head! Been shaken by earthquakes and nearly eaten by a giant megoroslug!"

Konrad looks up at Scrod and whispers something in his ear.

Scrod's eyes widen. "Double rations?" He thinks for a moment and then shouts. "Double? Nay, triple rations!"

Thompus raises one eyebrow, scratches his chin and looks up at the sky.

His paw lands on the rest with a slap. "You had me at double rations!"

"OK. Now we need a really good plan." Scrod turns very serious. "It's going to be extremely dangerous."

# Chapter 10

# A REALLY GOOD PLAN

The Vandal sits with its vents steaming as the Bilothians carry large barrels of sloshing water, sacks of purple fruit and bulging bags of fluff up the gangway and into the ship's hold. The rats and the Tingoils creep through the long grass, line up at the edge and watch. Rose pushes her snout through and sniffs the air. "How do we get back on board?"

Uphrasia's eyes narrow. "The same way we came out!"

"Coast is clear." Scrod hops out and marches toward the ship.

They all scamper over to the garbage hatch. Konrad stands on Scrod's shoulders and pulls hard on a handle. "Argh! It's stuck."

Nute cheers him on. "Pull, Konrad, pull!" Konrad glances down at her, then, with a mighty groan, he pulls the hatch handle. It gives way and Konrad swings under the ship hanging onto the hatch as a huge pile of slimy, smelly green goo falls on top of Scrod.

Rose sticks out her tongue and gags. "Yuck, even for a rat that's disgusting."

Scrod shakes off the slime. "Why is it always me who gets the most grimed? Never mind, up you go, smallest first."

The Tingoils climb up his back and hop in through the hatch. Then the others follow and haul Scrod up after them with his legs waggling. Inside the dank and filthy garbage hanger, Fazool stands next to a hatch, taps a code on a key pad and the hatch jerks open. They all follow him through the hatch and it slams shut behind them. Uphrasia punches the palm of his paw. "Of course. This is your ship. Those rotten blobs must have stolen it!"

Scrod wipes his fur, cleaning off the stinky green slime. He licks his paw and grooms behind his ears. "Nute, Thompus, go with Fazool. Find a way to communicate with the humans and warn them of their imminent destruction!"

Thompus and Nute stand to attention. "Sir, yes sir!" Fazool beckons them with his tiny claw and they follow. Scrod shakes his fur and the others guard their faces from the drops of slime. "Konrad, Rose, Uphrasia, Kazouri and Metnaz, your mission: sabotage that laser weapon!"

Konrad frowns. "What about you, sir?"

Scrod punches his paw and rubs his fist. "I have unfinished business with that despicable blob!"

On the bridge, Bibulous sits at his station. He operates the controls as the ship blasts away from the planet. Suddenly his antenna starts to wobble. He spots a flashing red light on his console. He flicks a switch and the screen flickers, then Konrad, Rose and Uphrasia appear with the Tingoils moving through a corridor. Bibulous spins around in his chair. "Crew! We have intruders aboard. Arm yourselves! Scour the ship. Look for and vaporise anything that moves!" The crew scurry about grabbing laser pistols and rifles from their lockers and begin loading them with power cells. Then they exit, hopping through various hatches that swish open then shut behind them.

Nute, Thompus and Fazool sneak along a corridor hugging the wall. They arrive at a metal spiral staircase. Tark and Gark start to descend, their heavy feet clunking on the metal steps. "I'm going to vaporise them!" Tark boasts.

"I'm going to obliterate them!" Gark retorts.

"I'm going to squish them then I'm going to macerate them!"

"Well I'm going to crush them, slice and dice them, then I'm going to flush them!"

Tark pauses on the bottom step. "Flush them. I like that. Yeah! Let's flush them! He, he, he!" They enter the corridor and look around. "Herm! Where are they?

"Bibulous said they were here on this level."

"I don't see them. Is it possible Bibulous imagined them?"

Gark holsters his laser pistol. "Well he has been under a lot of stress lately."

"Yes. Indicative of a latent dictator syndrome stemming from a lack of a patriarchal influence in his early child hood."

"Couple that with his abandonment issues, his paranoid and psychotic acting out of a subconscious maniacal-monster identity and what do you get?"

"Somebody who needs a lot of love!"

"Exactly." Tark holsters his weapon. "We should go and give him a hug."

"Or we could go down to the galley and eat our secret stash of fluff."

"I like your plan better. Let's go!" With that they both walk off along the corridor and exit through the hatch at the far end.

Thompus, Nute and Fazool drop down from the underside of the spiral staircase. Nute starts to climb the stairs. "Phew! That was a lot easier than I expected."

"Surprise, suckers!" Gark and Tark re-appear at the entrance to the corridor and start blasting with their laser guns. Thompus and Fazool race up the spiral staircase after Nute as bolts of white light bounce off the metalwork and hit the back wall leaving smouldering melted holes.

Tark holsters his weapon. "We missed them."

"It was your fault! You shouldn't have shouted out and warned them!"

"What did we discuss? We clearly agreed to shout out and surprise them!"

"Well I don't remember agreeing to shouting out that's all I'm saying."

Uphrasia, Konrad, Rose and the other Tingoils make their way up to the laser weapon. They find themselves in a network of corridors lined with lockers, sleeping quarters, a dining area and the ship's galley. Rose looks at a map on the wall. Metnaz points to the top of the map where the laser weapon is located. "We have to go three levels up, then all the way to the front of the ship. We have to pass by the bridge that way. Much too risky. Then up two levels through the air ducts. What's this?" Rose points to a spot on the map.

Kazouri looks over her shoulder and blows a raspberry.

"Ah... The toilets. So this area just next door must be the sewage treatment tank. There's a hatch on the top we can go through here up into the top level."

"Seriously! Through the sewage?" Uphrasia shakes his head. "Surely there's another way.

"Come on, we're rats. How hard can it be? It's the only way to avoid the bridge and detection."

They stand in a small cramped room looking at a hatch on top of a big blue pipe. Uphrasia starts to unscrew the hatch wheel and pulls it open. They all look away and grimace. "Phew! You cannot be serious! It stinks to high stilton!"

Rose hops up onto the pipe. "Just hold your breath and don't swallow anything!" With that, she holds her nose, jumps into the hole and, with a splash of dirty brown water, disappears inside the pipe. She swims along it and exits into the large sewage tank. She kicks off the wall with her back paws and swims upwards. Konrad is next. He swims as fast as he can through the pipe and up towards the top of the tank.

Uphrasia looks at the Tingoils and smiles. "After you guys." One after the other they both hop up onto the pipe and without hesitation jump in through the hatch. Uphrasia climbs up onto the pipe. "I'll never moan about taking a bath again!" He holds his nose and mouth with both paws and hops in. Inside the sewage tank the five swim upwards through the murky brown water. Rose reaches the upper hatch where there is a pocket of foul-smelling air. She starts to unscrew the hatch wheel. It's stiff and she struggles. Konrad arrives spluttering and coughing, he tries to assist her but the wheel still won't give. Uphrasia swims upwards passing the Tingoils and various suspicious-looking objects floating around in the sewage soup. A small blob shape turns and follows him upwards in ripples, shortening its body then growing longer in short pulses. Uphrasia coughs and chokes on every vile-smelling breath as he reaches the top. He helps them with the hatch wheel; with a creak it turns slowly. Then the Tingoils arrive and gasp for air.

The hatch opens into a dark grubby room with old rusty pipes and off cuts of cable strewn all over the floor. They all climb out and shake off the sewage water. Uphrasia takes off his tunic and wrings it out. "That was it! That was the most disgusting moment of my whole life! It's official!" He starts to put his tunic back on. Attached to his back is a leech. Its body is pale white with red blood vessels running from top to bottom. He buttons up the tunic and does not notice a piece of toilet paper stuck to his left ear.

Konrad stares at it. "You've got a thingy."

"What?"

"On your ear, a whatsit."

Uphrasia looks upwards then shakes his head and the toilet paper flies off. "Whoa, yuck!" He shudders.


The cargo hold is dark and in the corner on the floor is a round hatch. The circular handle starts to turn and the hatch opens a crack. Thompus pokes his sandy-brown snout through and sniffs three times. He opens the hatch fully and climbs out followed by Nute and Fazool. They scamper to the back of the hold and hide behind some packing crates. Nute feels the back wall. "It's hot here!"

Thompus feels the wall. "The engines must be just on the other side."

"That gives me an idea." Nute takes off her rucksack and rummages inside. Another hatch on the far wall swishes open and Carak and Spigot hop in with their laser rifles ready. They move around the cargo hold looking behind crates and shoving aside tool trolleys. Nute, Thompus and Fazool sneak along behind a low crate towards the hatch Carak left open.

"Psst!" Spigot stops in his tracks and looks over at Carak who nods his head sideways indicating a gap between two large crates at the back. They both move into the centre of the room and aim their weapons at two glowing eyes in the darkness. Carak narrows his eyes. "Ready?"

Spigot aims carefully. "Ready."

"Fire!" They both let forth and bolts of white light dart out of their rifles and hit the space between the two glowing eyes. There is a loud bang and an explosion of fire knocks them onto the floor. The glowing eyes on the back wall are two of Nute's calcite crystals, the heat from the ship's engines making them glow. The three sneak out through the hatch.

As Nute exits she looks back at the two unconscious Bilothians on the floor.

"Thermoluminescence!"

They stand in a short corridor with two doors on either side and one at the far end in front of them that leads to the bridge. Fazool indicates the door at the left and they enter. Nute looks around the tiny cramped communications room on the left. Many lights on the numerous consoles glitter and flash. Fazool hops up onto a tall chair in front of a monitor. Nute stands to his left, wrinkles her snout and frowns. "Looks complicated."

Thompus steps up to the right of Fazool. "He seems familiar with it all." He waves his paws over the dials and switches. "How do we send a signal to our ship?"

Fazool chirps and whistles and operates the transmitter, his hard claws tip-tapping away at the keyboard. Lights flash and the screen comes to life. Star systems appear and change, until an image of the Patrick Moore arrives on the screen. Fazool smiles. "Fazool…"

Nute hops up and down. "That's it – that's it!" Fazool turns a dial and a speaker under the screen crackles and buzzes. Faint human voices chatter across the airwaves. Fazool exchanges places with Thompus who takes the seat and looks at Nute, his face serious.

"Now the hard bit. I need you to connect my dome to the communications circuit."

"Will it hurt?" She strokes her wires remembering her horrible experience of human experimentation from her childhood.

"It will hurt, but we have to try don't we? I mean, I'm no hero but there is no other way to communicate with them. Is there? Once more unto the breach dear friends!"

Nute scrunches up her snout, pulls her screwdriver out from her utility belt and gets to work unscrewing the control panel.

Rose marches along the duct with purpose. She stands under an overhead air duct looking pleased with herself. The others follow. At the back Uphrasia stops and leans on the wall feeling dizzy. Konrad waits for him. "Are you alright buddy?"

"Yeah, yeah. I'm fine. Just a little worn out I guess. He catches up with Konrad. On his back under his tunic is a large bulge; the leech is enjoying a good feast on his blood.

Konrad looks concerned. "Your snout is pretty pale."

"I'm OK. Let's get on with the mission."

They make a stack with Rose and Konrad at the bottom and Uphrasia on top. He takes out his screwdriver and undoes the air vent cover. As he works on the last screw he pauses for a moment, his eyes close briefly and his head rocks back. Then he corrects himself, undoes the last screw and the vent cover falls with a clatter onto the floor. He pulls himself up into the duct and, bracing his feet on the ledge either side, pulls the others up one by one. The vent heads horizontally for a few metres then curves up abruptly. They gather at the base of the vertical section and look up. It rises up very high until all they can see is darkness. Rose purses her lips. "It's going to be a tough climb folks. Are we all up for this?" They all nod. "OK. I'll go first then you all follow." She reaches up and grips the metal seam in the vent and starts to climb. The climb is as tough as Rose implied. They sweat and strain as they edge upwards a rat foot at a time. Rose reaches a horizontal cross junction and carries on. Uphrasia sweats profusely as he climbs past the junction. Then Konrad reaches it. Something lands on his snout. He wipes it off with his paw and looks at it. It's blood. Uphrasia's eyes droop and close. His nose is pale. Then he collapses and falls ricocheting off the sides of the duct down towards Konrad. "Konrad look out!" shouts Rose.

Uphrasia stops with a jolt in mid-air. Konrad's left paw grips onto Uphrasia's wrist. "Got you!" He heaves Uphrasia up and swings him into the horizontal junction where he lands on his chest, limp and lifeless. Konrad hops in closely followed by Rose.

"What's this?" She pulls up his shirt and reveals the fat bloated leech attached to his back. "It's some kind of parasite?"

The Tingoils tip tap along the duct. Rose starts to pull the leech off. A Tingoil's hand stops her. Kazouri shakes his head and pushes her aside. Metnaz rummages in Rose's rucksack and takes out a short length of rope. He ties it to the tail of the leech, then to a vent in the duct ceiling and hauls it up in the air. Then he and Kazouri start to wind the rope round the top of the leech, round and round moving down so that the blood is pumped back into Uphrasia's body. The leach gets squeezed tighter and tighter by the rope and is soon completely wrapped up. Then the leech releases Uphrasia who flops down and groans.

Konrad turns him over and sits him up. "Uphrasia! Uphrasia!!

"Is it supper time?" He mumbles.

"That's my rat!" Konrad rubs his back. "Come on, wake up buddy."

Uphrasia opens his eyes. "Oh! I have the mother of all headaches!"

"Are you OK?"

"Yes I feel surprisingly good actually." He stands up and stretches. "I feel like I could run a marathon right now!" He starts to jog on the spot and heads forward then falls flat on his face.

Konrad helps him up again. "Take it easy pal. Let's climb that duct for now. You can run that marathon later."

They all climb out into the vertical duct again and start to climb.

Thompus' face is calm and serene as Fazool and Nute attach wires to his memory chip. Nute hops down while Fazool taps away on the console and the dome on Thompus' head starts to glow. Beads of sweat start to pour down his face and his body starts to stiffen. The dome changes from a green glow to a red glow and Thompus starts to shake. "Ah...!"

The computer's voice is dull and monotone. "Downloading salutations in all known languages." Thompus' teeth chatter and he shakes even more violently. "Downloading communication manual and commands." The dome begins to flash red to yellow.

"Download complete!" The dome fades and Thompus flops and slides off the chair onto the floor. Nute unplugs the wires and props him up. "Thompus? Are you still with us?"

Thompus groans and his eyelids open slowly. "Bonjour. Bueno Diaz. Subax wanaagsan!" He opens his eyes and grins. "Howdy!" Nute helps him to his feet and he climbs back up onto the chair. He flexes his fingers and starts to type away on the keyboard.

On the bridge of the Patrick Moore, the captain dozes in his chair, mumbling in a plaintive tone in his sleep, "No more ship's biscuits, no more ship's biscuits, please..."

The communications officer spins round from his console looking alarmed. "Captain! We are receiving a signal, from an alien craft!"

The captain splutters awake. "Alien craft! Put it on the main viewer!" The screen fizzes then an image of the Vandal comes into focus. "Alien life forms! So I finally make first contact! Me, Egglebert Villeroy! The first human to make contact with a species from outer space!" Then the screen fuzzes again and Thompus appears. "Rats! How disappointing!" Thompus waves and taps away on the keyboard. The captain stands up staring at the main viewer. "Are you getting that coms?"

"Yes sir, it's coming through now." The communications officer's eyes widen and he turns slowly round. "Captain, this is incredible! It's a warning that we are about to be destroyed by a deadly laser weapon on board that alien spacecraft. They recommend evasive action. What are your orders?"

The captain shrugs. "Obviously a trick. You can't trust a rat! All they care about is stuffing their faces and stealing anything they can get their grubby little paws on. Tell him to get lost. I'm not being duped by a sneaky lying rat!"

On the Vandal's bridge Bibulous sits at his console attempting to target the Patrick Moore on the main viewer with the green cross-hairs. "Hold still, infernal tin can!"

Rose squeezes through a vent backwards, wriggling her bottom out. She tugs Uphrasia after her and he slides out onto the floor and sits against the wall drooling and grinning. Konrad follows headfirst and gets jammed halfway out. Rose tugs him and he pops out.

"Ta!"

"Welcome."

Uphrasia talks in a slurred voice. "Such a lovely afternoon for a stroll. The cherry blossoms look so lovely this time of year." His eyes go wide. "Don't smell the flowers! The flowers of forgetfulness!"

The corridor is clean and brightly lit with a line of lockers along one side. The Tingoils slide out of the

196

duct and they all stand around Uphrasia looking down at him. "He's out of his tiny mind," Rose observes.

"He'll be fine." Konrad pulls him up onto his feet. "Uphrasia! The mission. Remember!?"

"Oh yes the mission. Must not forget the mission." He points down along the corridor. "Is it that way? Come on Konrad lets save the universe!" He sets off down the corridor stumbling from side to side.

Carak and Spigot wake up on the cargo hold floor and look at the damage they have caused. "We better find the intruders! Carak hops up and helps Spigot to his feet. They go through the hatch in the far corner of the bay, climb the spiral staircase and race up the next two levels. They sneak along a corridor wall holding their laser pistols low. They arrive at a doorway and Spigot nods at Carak to go in while he continues along the corridor. Carak creeps past the line of tall lockers. The middle locker's door is missing and Konrad is at the bottom of it. Uphrasia and Rose are stacked up on top of him with Kazouri and Metnaz on the very top hugging each other. Carak arrives at the locker but does not notice them as he walks past. Uphrasia whispers. "Bloated chump."

Carak pauses, narrows his eyes and spins around looking left and right. There is nothing there. "Spigot was that you?"

Spigot answers from the corridor "Was what me?"

"Flatulent beach ball!" Uphrasia covers his mouth with his paw and giggles.

Spigot looks insulted. "How dare you Carak! I have great control of my wind!"

Carak looks surprised. "What are you talking about?" He turns and continues down the corridor.

"I'm talking about you! You blubber bundle of gyrating jelly!"

Carak becomes very angry and he turns round and aims his rifle.

"How dare you! I'm on the new slender-quack diet I'll have you know!" "You stupid skinny matchstick!"

Spigot pokes his head round the doorway. "Who are you calling a skinny matchstick?!"

Carak fires a shot over Spigot's head. "You!"

Spigot ducks and aims back. "No need to get personal! Bumblebee features!" Spigot fires three bolts of laser light at Carak's feet making him hop about. The last bolt grazes Carak's toe. "Right, you've had it, you fart factory!" Carak hops behind the locker and lets forth with his laser rifle and they exchange rapid fire at eachother. Then Carak grins. "OK Spigot! You win! Cease fire!"

Spigot narrows his eyes, his antenna lowers and covers his middle eye, there is a pop and the eye comes out and sits on the end of his antenna. He pokes the antenna round the edge of the door and looks left and right. "Only if you do first!"

They fire a barrage of shots off at each other again. In the locker Rose holds her paw over Uphrasia's mouth to stop him from making matters worse. Bolts of light whizz past the locker and a few close shaves fizz and melt scars in the edge of the metal. Suddenly a speaker crackles and Bibulous' voice booms. "All crew to the bridge! All crew to the bridge! Prepare to activate the Obliterator!" Carak and Spigot stop firing.

Carak's eyes bulge. "Obliterator! That's me!" They both dart off in opposite directions.

The rats and Tingoils hop down out of the locker and Uphrasia whistles. "Phew, that was fun!" Konrad tries to get out, but is stuck. Rose and Uphrasia pull his arms and he pops out.

"Thanks."

"Welcome" They both say together.


In the cargo hold Tark and Gark both look at the smouldering mess of dripping molten metal on the wall opposite. "Should we mention this to Bibulous?" Tark asks.

"I think not. The mood he's in today he might turn the Obliterator on us instead of the culprits."

"Best say nothing then."

"Yeah..."

They walk out through the hatch together.

"That's the first time you've ever agreed with me!"

"I never agree with you! I just let you think that I do." Gark grins.

The Vandal hurtles towards the Patrick Moore, then retro rockets blast and it slows down. All the Bilothians are back at their stations on the bridge. Carak and Spigot glare at each other. Bibulous operates his targeting station. His tongue hangs out of his mouth as he locks onto the Patrick Moore. "At last! Activate! Activate!!"

Carak looks confused. "The recycling? The ship's entertainment system? We could do with a little music." The others nod in agreement.

Bibulous looks at him and shakes his head. "Activate the Obliterator you floundering flotsam! The Obliterator!!" He turns back to his station, then has an afterthought. "Also the ship's entertainment system, we could do with a little music after all."

Mantovani?"

"No."

Spigot interjects, "Bert Kaempfert!"

"No, no, no!"

Tark shouts out, "Roberto Mann!"

Gark thumps him on the arm. "Klaus Wunderlich! Klaus Wunderlich!"

Bibulous hops down from his chair and puts his hands on his head. "What do you people listen to? All those suggestions are awful. It's like some kind of easy-listening nightmare! We listen to Gert Wilden or nothing!" They all moan and groan and Tark hits the play button and very cheesy music starts to play.

Bibulous rubs his hands together and climbs back up on his chair. "Good! Now activate the Obliterator!"

The outside hatch opens, the laser rises up out of the ship, glowing and buzzing, and the tip emits the regular zap, zap pulse.

Back on board the Patrick Moore, Coms' voice is high-pitched. "Captain, the ship has stopped and it looks like they are charging their weapons."

The Captain shrugs. "Send a message in all known languages. Get stuffed! Foolish rats. Do they really think they can trick me? Top of my year. Graduated with honours! Ha!" He presses his intercom button. "Kitchen! Where is my hot chocolate!?"

"Sending rude message captain." Beads of sweat pour down Coms' forehead. "In all known languages."

Bibulous chews on a long, gooey, red-and-green-striped space ration that hangs down from a transparent dispenser above his console. He smiles his most evil smile as the message appears on his screen. He speaks with his mouth full. "Ha! Foolish humans. Charge the Obliterator!"

Carak pulls the lever, nodding. "Charging the obliterator!"

Bibulous makes his best effort at a kindly, merciful face. "Not too much! Just a teensy, weensy little bit. I want to play with them a bit before we blow them to smithereens!"

"Yes Captain!"

The laser throbs and glows on top of the ship and the transparent turret turns slowly until it points at the Patrick Moore. Bibulous spins round and round on his chair then grabs his console. "Ooh! I feel dizzy." Then he screws up his face and grits his teeth. "Fire!"

The laser fires a short sequence of light bolts that dart through space and hit the Patrick Moore. The hull explodes in three places and one of the rocket thrusters blows up, blasting burning fuel out into space. The Patrick Moore's bridge is rocked, consoles explode and people dive onto the floor. The Captain lets out a shrill scream. "Run away! Evasive protocol 438, fire all thrusters! Get me out of here!" The ship's thrusters fire and the massive ship pulls away.

Bibulous dances around the bridge flapping his arms like a bird. "They are trying to escape! He, he! The fools are trying to escape! Charge the Obliterator again, half power. Take out their engines!"

Carak bobs up and down excitedly in his chair. "Yes, your grimness!" The laser starts to get brighter and brighter, humming and throbbing.

Bibulous hops up onto his chair and grabs the joystick, targeting the Patrick Moore again. "Fire all thrusters! Give chase! He, he...!"

The Patrick Moore starts to move away from the planet. The Vandal's engines blast and it starts to increase in speed when they suddenly go out and the ship comes to a halt.

"What's going on? Where are my engines?!"

Spigot taps a dial on his console then turns slowly around. "Captain the fuel pump is not functioning!"

"Tark! Gark! Go to the cargo bay and check on the fuel pump. Fix it! Go, go!" Tark and Gark run through the hatch, down the corridor and into the cargo bay. They both look at the hole in the back wall.

Gark puts his finger in the hole in his antenna. "What a mess!"

Tark slaps his hand down. "Cut that out, we have to fix it. Come on!"

Tark rolls a tool station on a trolley over to the hole. Gark pulls over a ladder and climbs up.

Tark pulls a lever switching off the fuel, he passes up a welder and Gark turns it on, lights the bright blue flame and starts to weld up the hole.

Uphrasia, Konrad and Rose, guided by the agitated Tingoils, reach the laser room and look up into the transparent turret at a tangled mess of coloured wires. Rose scratches her head. "There's never been a more important moment to stack up guys!" Rose climbs up onto Uphrasia's shoulders and Konrad climbs up on top of her. The Tingoils climb up Uphrasia and hang onto Rose to direct Konrad. They point at a thick orange wire and Konrad grabs it and tugs it down towards his mouth. Rose groans under his heavy weight. "Hurry up Konrad!" Konrad's sharp front teeth gnaw away at the plastic insulation revealing the shining copper core.

The bridge of the Patrick Moore is total chaos. Coms swings round in his chair. "Captain! Another message from the rats!"

"Tell them we surrender!"

"No, sir. I believe they are trying to help us! The message reads 'Attempting to disable weapon!'"

The bridge shakes again. The captain clings to his command chair. "Astonishing! Rats helping humans? It's unthinkable! Well, send a reply."

"What shall I send sir?"

"Help?!"

Scrod watches the Vandal crew at work from the air duct. He clenches his paws and his knuckles make a crunching sound. "Now, you despicable alien fiend, it's time for a rat reckoning!"

Konrad points out a green wire. "This one?" The Tingoils shake their heads. He points at a bright yellow one. "This?" Again they shake their heads, then squeak and chirp as loud as they can, pointing at the blue cable.

Bibulous manoeuvres his joystick and the green targeting crosshairs on the viewing screen move around over the Patrick Moore again. Then the crosshairs fix on their target and change from green to red. "Got you! Prepare to be obliterated!" He looks over at Carak. "Well?"

Carak taps the fuel dial. "Still nothing captain."

Gark finally finishes welding up the last part of the hole and Tark pulls the lever and the fuel starts to flow to the engines. There is a loud whirring sound, the Vandal's rockets light up again and it pulls away and chases after the Patrick Moore.

Konrad wobbles and points to a pale blue cable. "What about this one?" The Tingoils get excited, nodding and chirping. "I guess this is the one then." Konrad nibbles as fast as he can, exposing the wire. Then the Tingoils point at the orange cable. Konrad pulls the orange wire towards the blue one trying to make contact with the wire he has exposed, but they will not reach.

Uphrasia sweats under the strain. "I can't hold your weight much longer, Konrad!"

Konrad pulls as hard as he can but the wires just will not meet. Rose starts to wobble and the rat stack moves from side to side. "Do something quick!"

Konrad looks at the orange cable, then the blue. They're just a rat's bite apart. He opens his mouth, bites down on both wires and closes his eyes.

Back on the bridge, the aliens hustle and bustle at their stations. "Fire, fire, fire!" Bibulous shrieks!

Carak hesitates. "It's not fully charged yet, captain!"

"Fire! Useless nincompoop! That's an order!"

Carak shrugs. "You're the boss." He presses the fire button.

Konrad's hair stands on end. His body goes rigid and glows white. There is a loud zap, and he shakes and convulses.

The laser weapon glows for a short moment then fizzles out and the barrel droops down.

The stack collapses and Konrad lands lifeless on top of Rose.

On the bridge, there is a bright white flash. The weapon console explodes throwing the crew onto the floor. Bibulous stands up holding his head in his hands. "My Obliterator! What have you idiots done?!"

He is startled by a menacing voice behind him. "I think the blame lies elsewhere!" Bibulous spins round.

Scrod leaps up and knocks Bibulous to the floor. He punches him over and over as they roll around. Bibulous kicks Scrod in the stomach and sends him flying back. Scrod somersaults backwards, lands on his feet and steadies himself.

Bibulous huffs and puffs. "Foolish vermin! I will annihilate you!"

"Not this time. The reckless monster exterminator has arrived!" Scrod leaps onto Bibulous and bites his antenna.

"Argh!!! You fight dirty!"

"I'm a rat, go figure!" Scrod kicks Bibulous with both his hind legs and sends him crashing into the master console. There is a loud explosion and the panel bursts into flames.

A blast of rocket fire exits the engines and the Vandal starts to arc sideways towards the planet.

Bibulous charges at Scrod, who flips him over his shoulder and slams him onto the floor. Scrod pounces back on top of him and punches Bibulous over and over in the face. Bibulous flops down knocked out. Scrod rolls onto his back exhausted. "Ah! I'm way too old for this rough stuff!"

Konrad's eyes are closed as Rose and Uphrasia drag him out into the corridor. Uphrasia shakes him by the shoulders. "Konrad wake up! Please don't die, old friend. Not you!"

Rose stifles a tear. "He was so brave!"

Konrad smiles and opens one eye. Smoke rises from his ears. "I was brave? Like, I-deserve-a-medal brave?"

Uphrasia hops up and down and claps his paws. "He's alive!"

Konrad opens his other eye and grins a wide grin. They help him up. Rose brushes him down. "Look at your fur!"

Konrad looks down. His fur is pure white and the tips glow with an iridescent fibre-optic light. "Wow! I'm lit up like a Christmas tree!" The Tingoils laugh and roll around on the floor clutching their stomachs.

In the cargo bay Gark's hastily made repair starts to glow red, then there is a mighty boom! The kind of boom the Bilothians would have really enjoyed. The Vandal spirals round and round towards the planet with a trail of fire and smoke. The corridor rocks and shakes and tips to one side. They all slide along the floor and crash into the wall.

Uphrasia takes charge. "We'd better get to the bridge fast!"

The bridge of the Patrick Moore is in flames. Fire fighters blast the burning consoles with fire extinguishers. Engineers work manically, fixing damaged circuits. Coms helps the Captain who is on the floor hugging the base of his command chair. "Captain, we're safe now. The alien vessel has stopped pursuing us!"

"They did it? I'm saved! I mean, we're saved!"

On the Vandal, the rats run through the corridors in panic as an alarm pulses and a deep robotic voice announces "Warning! Entering planet atmosphere at incorrect angle. Destruction imminent!" They slide down a ladder and race through the flaming cargo bay. Thompus, Nute and Fazool exit the communications room and meet the others in the corridor.

Scrod is still on the bridge battling with the master console, trying to control the ship. The others hop in through the hatch. Nute looks at Bibulous' body unconscious on the floor, then she grabs Uphrasia's arm. "I don't want to die! Do something Uphrasia!"

Konrad takes hold of her paw. "Don't be afraid. We'll figure something out!"

Carak comes round and tries to help. "I'll re-route the fuel line, try to get power to the engines." He desperately taps away at his console while Scrod wrestles with the command controls. The engines splutter then come to life. Carak punches the air. "Yes!" The ship is still spinning towards the planet. The engines roar and it weaves around and does a loop the loop. The rats hang on to the metal beams.

Scrod pulls hard on the joystick. "The control is inoperative. We're caught in the planet's gravity field. I'm sorry folks it's too late. You'd better say your goodbyes."

Tears well up in Nute's eyes. "I didn't want to be a space recruit. I wanted to be a dancer!"

Konrad takes both her paws in his. "You can still be a dancer!"

"Who wants to dance with a girl with wires in her head?"

Konrad pulls her in close. "It would be an honour to nibble on your wires. I think you are the finest rat I have ever met." He takes her in his arms and hugs her tight.

Uphrasia shuffles about on his feet, embarrassed. "Well I never. Fancy that. What a turn up."

Rose grabs him. "Come here, you fool!" She swings him round suspending him just above the floor and kisses him.

Thompus looks at Scrod and raises one eyebrow. "Some, Cupid kills with arrows, some with traps."

The robotic voice warns again. "Burn up in twenty seconds... nineteen... eighteen... seventeen..."

The ship bursts through the clouds and hurtles downwards, glowing in a halo of fire.

The Tingoils gather together and hold onto each other.

"Sixteen... fifteen... fourteen..."

Rose's eyes widen and she hugs Uphrasia tightly. "This is it guys!"

"Thirteen... twelve... eleven..."

Uphrasia looks into Rose's eyes. "I always liked you, right from the start."

"Ten… nine…"

"Why didn't you tell me sooner?"

"Eight…"

"I was a fool!"

"Seven…"

Thompus holds his cheeks, wide eyed. "Are we actually going to die, for real this time?!"

"Six… five… four…"

The ship starts to overheat, now completely enveloped in a curtain of fire with a tail of black smoke behind. Gark and Tark wake up and hold on to each other in a panic.

"Three…"

Suddenly the room jolts and they are all thrown to the floor. All is quiet. Konrad lies on his tummy with his eyes tightly closed. "Are we dead yet?!"


The Patrick Moore blasts through the clouds with its long robot arm holding onto the Vandal's hull. The bright multi-coloured space anchor rises up in the sky above. The breaking rockets blast and the ship slows down.

Scrod looks up at the control console  screen and the Patrick Moore appears through the clouds of smoke. "It's the humans. They saved us!"

Uphrasia looks up at the big main viewer to see the ground still rushing up towards them. "Not yet! We're still coming in too fast!"

"At this speed we will all be smashed to pieces!" Carak warns.

Then Bibulous stands up. "Wait!" Scrod readies himself for another battle. "I surrender! Come with me all of you. I can save us!"

The Patrick Moore strains and creaks as it slows down. The long arm starts to bend and buckle and a metal girder snaps! The land rises up fast, then the arm breaks and lets go of the Vandal. The little ship falls away from the Patrick Moore and heads towards the green meadows below. Bibulous leads them down a spiral staircase at the back end of the ship. He taps on a keypad and a door swishes open.

Nute looks up at Carak. "What's in here?"

"I have no idea. This room has always been out of bounds for us!" They all enter the room and look on open-mouthed. The room is filled to the ceiling with huge white clumps of fluff.

Bibulous waves everyone in. "Quickly eat as much as to can, your bodies will be relaxed for the crash and the fluff will cushion the impact!" They all rush inside and he heads back and stands in the doorway.

Carak starts filling his mouth. "But what about you boss?!"

"Someone has to land this ship!" With that, Bibulous closes the door and heads back to the bridge. He straps himself into Carak's seat, slams his hand on the rocket thruster button and grabs the joystick.

In the fluff store Scrod grabs a big pawful and holds it up to his mouth. "Well you heard the blob! Eat as much as you can, quickly!" The breaking rockets fire. The ship rocks and wobbles. The ground gets closer and closer. All rats, Tingoils and the Bilothian crew are all fast asleep on the mountain of fluff.

The ship's computer starts to announce the coming crash. "Five thousand feet to impact..." Bibulous strains at the controls heaving back on the joystick! "Four thousand feet to impact..." He jams both his feet on the console, groans and strains! "Three thousand..." The rockets blast! The underside glows red hot. On the screen Bibulous sees a valley and he steers the ship through it between two rising cliffs towards a wide open lake. "Two thousand..."

Sweat pours off his forehead. "Argh...!" The ship swings from side to side and clips a rock smashing off one of the landing gear legs.

"One thousand..."

The ship darts down and crashes into the lake making a huge wake in its path. Then it is gone. The surface of the lake is once again still and all is quiet.

Then the water parts and the Vandal pops up to the surface. Water boils from the underside and steam rises up.

Apart from Bibulous they have all slept through the whole rescue. The Patrick Moore has towed the Vandal out of the lake and onto the shore. The human crew has carried Bibulous to their infirmary and repaired his broken leg and other injuries sustained in the crash.

After a few hours they all come round, yawn and stretch. Konrad scrabbles to his feet. "Are we all alive?! He runs about over the fluff mound shaking and checking on his shipmates. Then he arrives next to Thompus. "Phew-wee, what's that stink?!"

Thompus looks down. "Sorry about that. I seriously thought it was the end." He waves his paw over a steaming pile of rat poo.

They exit the fluff store and climb up the spiral stairs and out into the cargo hold. The hatch is already lowered so the rats and Tingoils exit followed by Carak and the alien crew. They walk out into the bright sunlight to find a large crowd of humans and rats waiting for them, including Bibulous sitting in a wheelchair with his leg in plaster. There is a huge cheer and a loud rapturous round of applause.

Nute touches Konrad's arm gently. "Now we are saved, do you still want to nibble my wires?"

Konrad smiles, takes one of her wires and nibbles the end of it. Nute clasps her paws and giggles.

Uphrasia puffs up his chest. "This truly is a momentous day for all ratkind!"

Rose stares at the humans and rats gathered together. "Is it possible, rats and humans, friends?"

They both look at Thompus, who shrugs. "I can't think of anything negative to say at this point, except. Merrily, merrily shall I live now Under the blossom that hangs on the bough."

The two groups walk towards each other, greet and shake hands and paws. Some of them even try to hug, although there is a huge size difference between rats and humans, so in this case it's more of a squeeze of a leg and a pat on the head.

The Bilothian crew rush over and hug Bibulous, who complains a lot. "Get off me! Stop that. Who kissed me? Pack it in!"

Uphrasia and Konrad both look very proud as they stand in a line next to General Scrod, Rose, Nute, Thompus and the three Tingoils. A large crowd gathers to watch as Captain Villeroy leans down and pins a shiny silver star onto Scrod's uniform. "Congratulations, General. You are the first Intergalactic Sherriff! Someone to make sure we all keep in line with our brand-new way of living together!" Villeroy pins a medal on the breast pocket of Uphrasia's uniform. "Uphrasia Teach, the medal of honour and a promotion to Captain! I am sure you will lead your team on many greater adventures!" Konrad's lower lip quivers as he receives his medal. "Konrad Konstantin! Our new chief of sabotage and guardian of stores and supplies!" Konrad raises his snout proudly. I must thank you for the brave and daring sacrifice you made to save our ship from destruction!" Rose is next in line and she grins from ear to ear. "Rose! Many congratulations on your promotion to First Officer! You have already shown great resourcefulness and skill." He then leans down and pins a medal on Nute's white coat. "Nute, our new Chief of Scientific Developments! I think our own ship could do with a science officer of your calibre." Then he pins a medal on Thompus' tunic. "And you, sir, you have shown much bravery in the face of so many dangers! I award you the Medal for Bravery!" Thompus looks left and right, confused, surely he means someone else. Then it's the turn of the Tingoils. "As for our new alien friends, I am pleased to announce that they have joined up with Space Corps and have granted Uphrasia Teach the role of captain of the Vandal!" Nute smiles with pride then puts her hand in her pocket and finds a small white envelope. She takes it out and reads the address on the front. Villeroy takes a step back and salutes them. "You brave few have shown us the way, unifying previously sworn enemies with a new way of living together for the betterment of both. A proud day for humans and for rats!" A great cheer goes up and all the other rats rush forward, lift the heroes up onto their shoulders and march them around singing their favourite song.

> "It's tough at the bottom of the food chain."
> "When every single day is do or die,
>  and whenever you look up,
>  all you see is someone's butt,
> crapping down on you from on high!
> Yes it's tough at the bottom of the
> food chain, when no one seems to
> care or wonder why. You're bound
> to stink a bit, when you're swimming
> round in shoo-ooh-oo-wage. The
> scorn of every single passer-by!"

The celebrations went on well into the night, and a whole lot of that purple fruit was eaten. There may have been a small food fight here or there, but not a bad word was ever exchanged between human and rat, at least not on this planet.

# Chapter 11
# RATOPIA

Nine busy and blissful months have passed and the planet surface is a hive of activity. A human farmer drives a tractor pulling a plough across a new field, while a line of rats wearing straw hats and white cotton tunics follow behind, throwing seeds into the furrows. New meadows stretch out into the distance populated by neat lines of young apple, pear and hazel trees. Rows and rows of vegetables cover another field and huge barrels are filled with strawberry plants that hang over the edges, bulging with luscious red fruit. At the edge of the meadow wooden bee hives are already buzzing with hard-working bees pollinating the flowers of the purple fruit trees. Perfect oblong fields of oats and barley blow in the light breeze and ripen under the shining Ratopian sun.

A steady stream of rats and humans file in and out of the Patrick Moore carrying equipment and supplies. Another line of rats carry clumps of purple fruit up to a table where Scout loads it into a mashing machine. The machine crushes the fruit and juice pours into a container below. A farmer rat slumps against it, drunk. He makes a loud burp!

Behind the ship a small settlement is under construction. Wood-framed houses swarm with men and rats hammering and sanding, painting and sawing. A line of young rats walk up and down a sloping beam with paws full of nails which they deliver to the human labourers. Next to this construction site are small rows of miniature versions of the same, individual rat homes already finished. Painted in various colours, each has a neat little garden in front and back. A mother sings softly as she spoon feeds a row of seven little kits on a long bench all wrapped in cotton, laying on a bed of soft white fluff.

A watermill sits next to a wide river with a waterwheel rolling round and round steadily to power the mill. Tark, Gark, Metnaz and Kazouri sit at a long table kneading bread. Gark picks up a large bread paddle and slides it under three loaves. He carries them over to a boiling-hot, wood-fired bread oven and slides them inside. Then he slides the paddle under three other loaves that are already cooked and takes them back to the table. They all raise their noses to smell the fantastic aroma of freshly baked bread.

Scrod and Fazool are busy repairing the Vandal. Scrod lies underneath, his paw reaching out and up. "Wrench?!"

Fazool hands him a screwdriver and says. "Wrench."

"No, the other wrench?"

Fazool hands him a wrench and smiles. "Other wrench."

On the bridge of the Vandal Uphrasia sits at the main console with Carak next to him going over the controls. He points at a button. "And this is the main viewer zoom?"

"Yes! Up to zoom in, down for out," Carak nods enthusiastically. "That button is for targeting and this one is lock on target."

"Ah yes." He moves the joy stick around and the crosshair on the screen moves over a view of the construction site." Uphrasia zooms in on a paint tin.

A human painter dips a brush into the paint pot and dabs it onto a window frame.

Uphrasia presses a red button. "This must be for lock off?"

Carak tries to stop him but it's too late. "No, that's fire!"

The laser weapon on the top of the ship fires a short bolt of white light and the paint tin is evaporated. The painter dips his paint brush unaware, then looks around puzzled. Where has it gone?

In the centre of the settlement is a large geodesic dome made out of white triangle shapes on a metal frame. A lab rat stands at the entrance door, taps a code into a key pad, the door opens and he enters. Inside a brand-new laboratory has been constructed and Nute sits at a high desk looking through a giant magnifying glass and solders a circuit board. On a large bench in the centre of the room is the remains of the Cybormoggy that Uphrasia defeated on the Patrick Moore. The head has been altered to look like a rat's and the body is laid flat on its back with panels open and the interior circuitry exposed. A team of lab rats beaver away at it, pulling out cables and reattaching circuit boards.

A few metres beyond the dome is a small school house with tall pillars supporting a thatched roof. The sides are open and rows of young rats sit listening intently to Thompus as he gives a lecture on bravery. "You see, when you are facing imminent death you must not show any fear! You have to be brave in the face of peril!" A small black rat raises her paw and Thompus nods at her.

"Is that how you defeated the deadly Bilothian captain sir?"

Thompus looks very smug. "Well it was a rough fight but I used my deadly fighting skills learned at astro school!" A young albino rat butts in.

"But I heard it was General Scrod who defeated the Bilothian captain sir?"

Thompus shrugs. "Well in the heat of battle it's hard to remember who battled with who. Let's just say it was a team effort!" He punches the air rather unconvincingly. "Kapow! And, yes, well… OK. That's all for today. Remember little ones, love all, trust a few, do wrong to none!" The young rats exit the school room and walk past a large mixed group of rats watching a cooking demonstration hosted by Konrad. He wears a white chef's hat and stands behind a table covered in ingredients and a large mixing bowl. He picks up the bowl and, using a wooden spoon, whips a creamy batter. "The key to the perfect ship's biscuit is not too much cinnamon! Next I will demonstrate megoroslug au vin." The crowd ooh and ah!

Rose marches along behind the crowd in a shiny new elite cadet's uniform, proudly wearing her first officer's insignia on her breast pocket. Eight rats march behind her in matching uniforms, including black rats, brown rats, fancy rats, an albino rat and a pair of Zucker rats. They march into a white-painted building with a shiny silver sign over the entrance: "Town Council." Rose takes her place at one of several raised tables set up in a semicircle. Six human representatives, including Captain Villeroy, sit at low tables in a semi-circle facing the rats. They discuss the important matters of business affecting the new community. A black rat raises her paw. Villeroy points to her and she speaks, "We need more sewers!" All the rats shout out, "Hear, hear!"

Villeroy writes down the request. "More sewers. Right."

"Plus, the main sewer should go directly under the rat's community with unlimited access for all rats to drains, manholes and flood vents."

Villeroy nods in agreement. "Unlimited access."

A brown rat adds. "You need to throw away more food waste!"

Villeroy looks confused. "But we try not to waste food."

Rose explains. "We prefer our food a little on the rotten side."

"I see." He thinks for a while then, "Perhaps we could create a food waste depot next to the rat's community."

All the rats nod and shout "Hear, hear!"

The rats and humans exit the building and they all look very pleased with the outcome of their council meeting.

Nute backs out of the geodesic dome with the other lab rats. She holds a remote control in her paws. Then the new Cyborat emerges into the sunlight. It walks on two feet with heavy, thudding footsteps. The eyes glow bright orange with new lenses Nute has made from the calcite crystals she collected. The Cyborat stops and sways a little back and forth. Scout hops up beside Nute looking nervous. "Is it s-safe?"

"Sure, although I have not activated the central core yet, I believe I have managed to reprogram the main hard drive and we have made a few positive image changes as you can see." The young school rats gather round to watch. Nute pushes her wires back over her head and takes a deep breath. "Here goes!" She presses a button and the Cyborat activates. The eyes start to flash and the jaw snaps open and shut three times. Then in a loud booming voice it shouts,

"Exterminate all vermin! Exterminate all vermin!" All the school rats run away squealing!

Thompus jumps into the town water well and clings onto the bucket. As he drops down the well rope unravels. There is a splash and a plaintive cry from within, "Help!

Nute taps away on her remote control and grins. "Oops I forgot to reset the voice memory. This should do the trick!" She flicks another switch and the Cyborat says in a softer voice "Rescue all rodents! Rescue all rodents!" It winds up the well handle and a soaking Thompus emerges looking very cross.

Later on Thompus sits beside a fire drying off and cleaning out water from his ears. A pair of human feet arrive and stand next to him. He looks up to see Professor Fenkle standing over him. Thompus drops his towel.

"Please don't be alarmed, I mean you no harm." Fenkle smiles a crooked smile.

Thompus scowls up at him. "You tortured me!"

"Ah yes. I must apologise for that but you have to admit the food was good!"

Thompus raises his eyebrows and nods. "Yes I guess the food was rather good."

"I was wondering if we could come to terms?"

"Terms?" Thompus picks up the towel and dries his feet. "What terms?"

"You have some rather sensitive files in your memory chip I would very much like to have returned."

Thompus grins. "Oh yes! Those embarrassing pictures."

Fenkle fans his hands up and down. "Yes. Well let's keep this between us shall we?"

"Well what do you have to trade?"

"Whatever you like my dear little friend."

Thompus scratches his chest. "There are a few movies on the ships memory banks I'd like to see."

"Movies?"

"Yes. The Bubonic Plague, Rats' Night of Terror, Ben and Rodentz. There are loads more."

"What a splendid idea! I love a good horror movie. How about you come over to my place and Ilonja will make you a splendid dinner? Then we can watch these rat movies on my big screen!"

"I suppose the food will be very good?"

"Ilonja is a master chef! I can guarantee the food will be top notch, and I promise not a hint of torture."

Thompus smiles. "To be or not to be, that is the question. I'm in!"


After just twelve months most of the settlement is fully constructed and people begin to get on with their lives. A market has sprung up in the town centre and Scout is doing a roaring trade selling a bottled version of his boozy purple drink to the humans. The first harvest has come in and all sorts of vegetables and home produce are on sale. The Tingoils have a bakery stall and a large queue forms for their latest speciality: a purple wholemeal loaf. Gark and Tark wanted to set up a stall together but they are still arguing about what to sell.

All the school rats sit at a long wooden table for a lunchtime banquet. The Cyborat waits on them bringing tray after tray of delicious food: purple fruit pies, freshly baked bread courtesy of the Tingoils and a selection of Konrad's culinary creations, including ship's biscuits, of course.

Away from all this activity is a lush green meadow. Insects buzz and zizz in the long waving grass. Uphrasia and Rose lie on their backs in the sun, eyes closed, paws clasped together. Uphrasia beams a wide smile at her. "This is so much better than in my dreams."

"Yes, we actually found our Ratopia, didn't we?" She nestles close to him and nuzzles her snout in his fur.

"We sure did. It will be nice to settle down here."

"How many kits will we have?"

"Oh. At least thirty in the first litter."

She jabs him in the ribs with her elbow. "Hey I'm not popping out thirty kits. No way!"

They both look up into the sky and close their eyes.

Konrad's voice shouts in the distance "Uphrasia!"

"Oh bother, what is it now?" Uphrasia stands up and looks left and right.

Uphrasia and Rose emerge from the tall grass to find Konrad and Thompus standing next to the Vandal wearing their spacesuits. Uphrasia stops smiling. "What's going on, guys?"

Konrad places his right foot on his space helmet and puffs up his chest. "Space travel, danger, the unknown. Everything we signed up for at Space Corps buddy."

"You're leaving?"

"Yes, my friend, we are going on another adventure!"

Uphrasia's mouth turns down at the sides. "What about Ratopia?"

Nute steps out of the Vandal and walks down to Uphrasia. She puts her paw in the pocket of her lab coat, pulls out the letter and gives it to him. "Grandfather slipped this into my pocket. I think he meant to give it to you. When the time was right." Uphrasia looks shocked as he reads the familiar paw-writing on the envelope. He walks over to the well and leans against it. The Cyborat's heavy metal feet thud up the gangway carrying a large crate of bottles containing purple juice.

As Uphrasia reads the letter a change comes over his face, like a great weight has been lifted.

*My dear Son,*

*I am so sorry I cannot be with you today. You must have had many questions to ask me as you were growing up, none of which I could answer as I was so far away from you and my beloved wife.*

*If you are reading this, then my good friend Jonas Abler will have kept his promise and encouraged you to seek a life of adventure and exploration. A dangerous but eventful life; and by now I am sure you will know the great rewards it can reveal. Of course, if you are reading this note then I am not with you. I have not returned as planned from my own adventure to bring you and Margaret to a new home in the stars.*

*My plan was to head for the Crab Nebular in the hope of finding somewhere to settle. No doubt I am dead or lost in space; either way I want you to be brave, courageous and strong. After all it is in our nature as rats to explore and seek adventure and despite the risks, it would be a shame not to follow your destiny.*

*Perhaps one day we may meet again and you can tell me all about your own wonderful travels.*

*Please know that not a day goes by when I don't think of you. I will always be proud of you and love you.*

*Your father,*
*Edward Teach.*

Uphrasia frowns and looks up at Konrad with watery eyes. Rose puts her paw on his shoulder. "It would be a shame to miss out on all that adventure and danger, don't you think?"

He looks at her aghast. "You too?"

She throws out her arms. "Space travel! Life-threatening situations! Diabolical aliens! Asteroid storms!" She raises her eyebrows and tilts her head.

Uphrasia rubs his chin. "Well..."

Scout arrives carrying a large box and gives it to Konrad.

Konrad grins. "Captain Villeroy has given us his whole supply of ship's biscuits. Seems the humans aren't so keen on them."

Uphrasia jumps into the air and claps all four paws together. "I'm in!"

As they all board the Vandal, Uphrasia and Rose pause at the top of the gangway and look back at the bustling scene. Rose sighs. "It's going to be a beautiful little town. Scrod stands on the gangway of the Patrick Moore wearing a smart black shirt with his bright shining silver star on his chest. He beams a warm smile, waves them farewell and they wave back. Rose squeezes Uphrasia's paw. "You don't mind leaving Ratopia?"

He kisses her gently on the forehead, looks into her eyes and smiles. "You're my Ratopia."

The Tingoils and the Bilothians operate the controls, all sporting brand-new Space Corps uniforms. Carak instructs Nute on how to operate the controls of his station. Uphrasia sits in the command chair looking through space charts with Fazool. He talks into a microphone on the command console "Bibulous! Don't be all day down there!"

In the ship's galley Bibulous is washing up a huge pile of dishes in a big metal sink. He has a bandage on his injured antenna where Scrod bit him. "This is so demeaning. One of these days!" He shakes both his fists, then winces and strokes his antenna. "Ouch."

The cargo hold is full of boxes, some labelled "Ship's Biscuits" others containing supplies and equipment. Konrad and Metnaz check off the inventory as Kazouri stacks yet more crates of ship's biscuits onto the shelves. Rose is in the engine room overseeing Tark and Gark as they make welding repairs to the fuel lines. Thompus in the meantime is outside painting a new sign on the side of the ship. Underneath the words "The Vandal" he has painted a Space Corps logo with "Frontier Rats" in smaller letters underneath. Down in the fluff store, in the darkest corner of the room, a pair of red eyes glow in the centre of a feint outline of a Cybormoggy's head.

All the crew gather on the bridge. There is an air of excitement as they make their final checks. Fazool sits next to Uphrasia on the command console and Kazouri and Metnaz assist the constantly arguing Gark and Tark. Nute and Carak operate the long range scanners. Carak looks over to Uphrasia. "What's our destination Captain?"

Uphrasia looks at the screen for a moment then smiles. "Enter co-ordinates for the Crab Nebular!"

"Are we going to blow it up?" Carak grins.

"No! What is it with you? We're not blowing anything up. Just set the course."

Carak sulks as he taps away at his console and under his breath says. "No fun anymore, no explosions, no kaboom."

The cargo door is raised up and seals with a hiss. The engines ignite and roar and jets blast downwards from the underside lifting the ship up vertically. Then the Vandal blasts up into the blue sky in an arc of vapour. It vanishes into the clouds then re-appears above the planet. The engines roar, rising in volume and pitch. Then in a blinding flash it darts off into space getting smaller and smaller until it is just a tiny speck.

THE END

# About the writer

I grew up one of six children raised by our Mother in a tiny two-bedroom cottage in the West Country. I developed a deep interest in nature and the wild creatures that lived in the unspoiled countryside around us. As a child I was a big fan of writer Gerald Durrell and developed my own menagerie of animals including four bantam hens, fourteen rabbits, budgerigars and a dog.

At six years old I would sneak out of bed and creep down stairs after everyone had gone to sleep to watch movies on our old black and white TV. It was no wonder I could not concentrate at school and was a late starter when it came to reading. After the incident when I released the school budgerigars I was politely expelled.

I rent a small chalet on the Dorset coast that I use as my escape from city life and in the off season to hide away and write in peace. Much of this novel was conceived and written there in between long walks along the coast.

86009212R00130

Made in the USA
Columbia, SC
24 December 2017